GLOM
GLOOM

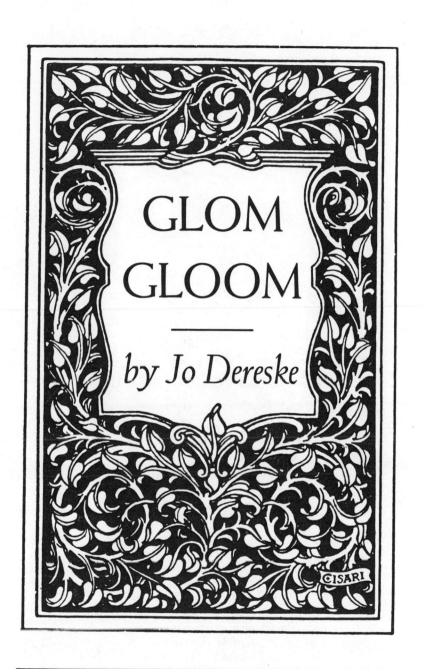

GLOM GLOOM

---

by Jo Dereske

ATHENEUM · NEW YORK 1985

Library of Congress Cataloging Publication Data

Dereske, Jo.   Glom gloom.

SUMMARY: No one remembered the old rhyme about
the Garter Gates until Raymond Fibbey and his friends
discovered the danger that lay behind them.
1. Children's stories, American. [1. Fantasy]
I. Title.
PZ7.D4418GL   1985   [Fic]   85-7451
ISBN 0-689-31131-1

Published simultaneously in Canada by
Collier Macmillan Canada, Inc.
Composition by Dix Type, Inc. Syracuse, New York
Printed and bound by Fairfield Graphics,
Fairfield, Pennsylvania
Designed by Mary Ahern
First Edition

For Karen and Erik

Contents

And now remember the Gartergates,
Full three times Glom Gloom high,
When Strong they be, no harm to ye,
But left to lie, prepare to die.

from the Bulking legend
of Glom Gloom

1 · Gloom Day

OOD GLOOM!"

"And Good Gloom to you," the Bulkings called out cheerily to one another in the brightly decorated Mid-cobbie of Waterpushin.

It was Gloom Day. Old grudges and bad feelings were forgotten in the celebration of the season's greatest holiday. This day was set aside to remember the great Glom Gloom, the Finder of Waterpushin. It was not a day to be stingy with one's friendliness.

Red and yellow holiday colors were everywhere. The Bulking women swirled their red and yellow holiday cloaks about them as they walked. Red and yellow arm bands showed on the men's tunic sleeves as they waved and greeted each other.

Bulking children in cleverly sewn red and yellow costumes flitted from booth to booth, running around and between the adult Bulkings. Faces wore sugary stickiness from popsies and sweetcakes.

The Mid-cobbie of Waterpushin was as transformed by Gloom Day as the Bulkings. Instead of the quiet village shops that opened onto the Mid-cobbie, there were bright holiday booths, painted and decorated in red and yellow. Booths that sold sweetcakes and popsies and more sweets and rich, spicy breads. Booths with jewelry and tiny treasures and clever toys. Booths of games: Spinney, Jackins, ball throwing.

"Step over here!"

"Try your luck at Spinney!"

"Come and see-ee. See-ee what I have!"

There were holiday singers strolling about the Mid-cobbie, pausing to sing the old songs of the great Glom Gloom and the flight from the Weeuns into the safety of Waterpushin.

In the square, close to the Majester's house, there was a small stage with puppets. Acrobenders and jugglers performed to wide-eyed children wherever they could find an empty space. All around the square there were more booths.

All the Bulkings in the valley were in Waterpushin celebrating Gloom Day. They jostled one another good-naturedly as they made their way from booth to booth, from event to event, carrying their purchases and eating the special Gloom Day foods.

Raymond Fibbey slipped between the slow-moving Bulkings and hurried from booth to booth, pausing just long enough to glance at the wares. He didn't care much about the jewelry or the trinkets. He would have liked a sweetcake or a popsie, but his money was gone.

Raymond's mother had given him five pennies after breakfast, but he'd spent them at a ball-throwing booth in the square.

One penny for three balls. Two of the three balls had to be tossed into a vegetable basket. Raymond had been sure he could throw the balls into the basket and win one of the caps that hung on the back and side walls of the booth. The Bulking in the booth said the deep green caps were like the great Glom Gloom's cap. Raymond had never seen a cap on any of the drawings of Glom Gloom. He didn't believe the Bulking, but he still wanted one of the caps for his own.

But each time, two of the three balls had bounced out of the vegetable basket. Five times he tried, and five times he lost, and then his five pennies were gone.

"It's a shame, it is," the Bulking in the booth had said, shaking his head.

Raymond didn't believe him then, either.

"Gloom Cakes! Gloom Cakes! Only one penny. Fine Gloom Cakes. Get them he-ere," sang a huge, red-nosed Bulking. He stood in front of a yellow booth decorated with red stars and moons, holding up a tray of decorated sweet-cakes.

A woman wearing a flour-covered apron worked inside the booth. Raymond stopped and watched her mix the sweet dough in a large wooden bowl. Then she rolled it out with a wooden rolling pin, sprinkling flour on the dough as she rolled. A flat pan was lined with cut shapes, ready to pop into the oven at the back of the booth. Baked shapes were cooling on one end of the long table, waiting to be decorated with the rich red and yellow sugar frosting.

The red-nosed Bulking held up a Gloom Cake from his tray. It was in the shape of Glom Gloom with his crooky-staff over his shoulder.

"Fine Gloom Cakes!"

He held up another sweetcake in the shape of a Weeun, a tiny figure all hunched over, with fear painted on his face in bits of yellow sugar frosting.

"None other like them! Get them he-ere!"

Even if he had had a penny, Raymond didn't think he could eat the noble figure of Glom Gloom. It was too real, too proud. But the sweet smell of the Gloom Cakes made Raymond's stomach rumble.

3

The woman in the booth moved to the other end of the long table and began to decorate the baked and cooled sweetcake figures.

Raymond eased closer to the booth, closer to the bowl of sweet Gloom Cake dough the woman had left sitting on the end of the long table closest to him. There was a counter of boards built all around the booth, but if he pushed himself on his stomach across the counter he might be able to reach the bowl of dough . . .

"Angus!" the woman screeched. "Look to what the rascal's doing!" She pointed a spoon of red sugar frosting at Raymond.

Raymond was lying across the counter with his feet in the air. By stretching out his arm he was able to scoop up a handful of the fragrant dough. He jumped back as the woman screamed, "Robbery! Robbery!"

In his haste to be after Raymond, the Gloom Cake man missed setting the tray of Gloom Cakes on the counter. They fell to the cobbie, scattering in front of the booth. There was barely a chance for the Gloom Cakes to reach the ground before the Bulking children standing nearby grabbed them up and ate them, gobbling broken bits of Glom Gloom and the Weeuns and giggling at their good fortune.

"Let me through," the red-faced Gloom Cake man shouted at the crowd that had gathered.

"Let him be," said a voice from the crowd. "That was Raymond Fibbey and you'll never catch him. He knows every hidey-corner in Waterpushin."

"Aye," said another voice. "Raymond's a troublemaker, but he'll not be caught today. Asides, it's Gloom Day. Let him go."

"Yes. Let him go. It's Gloom Day," the crowd agreed, nodding to one another and to the Gloom Cake man.

The Gloom Cake man looked around at the faces in the crowd. He threw up his arms in disgust.

"All right, it's Gloom Day. I'll let him be."

The crowd laughed good naturedly in approval.

"I'm thankful he's not my own," said the Gloom Cake woman.

"There's not a father or mother here who doesn't agree with you," said the first man who'd spoken.

"Raymond's enough to send a mother crying in the night," added a woman carrying twinling girls, one on each arm.

Raymond dodged through the crowd that was watching the Gimly School girls dancing around a tall trunk vine. The trunk vine represented the crooky-staff of Glom Gloom. Tall and stately, its length was carved with flowers and animals.

Raymond broke stride just enough to take another bite from the diminishing ball of Gloom Cake dough. It was rich and sweet and sticky. He would have liked to make it last a long time, but it tasted too good.

He squeezed into the center of the crowd watching the stick figure show in the square. A small stage had been set up at the end nearest Majester Trader's house. The stage was bright yellow with red streamers and a red curtain. The Bulkings sat and stood in a semi-circle around the stage, the smallest in front. Behind the red curtain, someone was pulling strings to make the stick figures move about the stage.

"I will lead you away from the Weeuns so we can live free forever," a voice said from behind the curtain, and the stick figure of Glom Gloom jerkily raised its crooky-staff above its head.

"Glom Gloom! Glom Gloom," the children shouted in excitement.

Raymond remembered only a season or two ago when he had been like them, so excited by the stick figures that he almost believed they were real.

He searched through the crowd for the red nose of the Gloom Cake man. Licking the last of the dough from his fingers, he decided he was safe. No one had come after him.

He wandered through the brightly decorated square, stopping to watch an acrobender double backwards as he balanced on top of a spinning wheel.

He was held for a few minutes by a juggler tossing red and yellow dyed eggs in arcs above his head. The juggler claimed he was juggling raw eggs. Raymond gave a loud, piercing whistle just as the juggler had four eggs in the air at once. The juggler jerked in surprise, and the eggs fell onto the smooth stones of the square. They bounced and rolled into the crowd, but none of them broke. The crowd laughed and hooted. The juggler stood red-faced, looking around for whoever had whistled.

"You are not for true," Raymond shouted and ran away.

He wondered just how much of any of Gloom Day was for true. Was Glom Gloom for true? Had he really been a noble Finder, a rescuer? Or was he just made up so the Bulkings could celebrate a holiday? And who had ever seen a Weeun? All anyone seemed to know about the Weeuns was the old legend everyone had to memorize in school about Glom Gloom mysteriously defeating them.

6

The legend ended:

And now remember the Gartergates,
Full three times Glom Gloom high.
When strong they be, no harm to ye,
But left to lie, prepare to die.

And what about the Gartergates? If there really was such a thing as the Gartergates, no one Raymond knew cared whether they were strong or left to lie. In the old stories, the Gartergates had been built by the Finders to forever protect the Bulkings and the valley of Waterpushin from the evil Weeuns. If the Gartergates were supposed to keep the Weeuns out of Waterpushin, who knew if the Gartergates were still strong, or even standing; or for that matter, where they were?

Raymond kicked at an empty Sweetun bottle lying in his way.

"Ow," someone in front of him cried out.

Raymond slipped to the edge of the Mid-cobbie so that whoever had been hit by the bottle wouldn't see him.

"Ah, Raymond," said a voice beside him. "Trouble seems to follow you like the tail on a mouseling, doesn't it?"

It was Gos, the pot mender, leaning on his rickety old pushcart. In honor of Gloom Day, Gos had tied ribbons at two corners of the sagging canopy over his pushcart. One ribbon was yellow and the other a dull orange.

"How would you know?" Raymond asked, reaching out to touch a shiny miniature of Glom Gloom lying among a helter-skelter of fine silvery Tinies.

Gos lifted his walking stick and smartly tapped Raymond's knuckles. Raymond jumped back and rubbed his stinging hand.

"I'm not blind, my boy," Gos said. "And asides, don't you think I have ears in my head? I hear how Raymond Fibbey's mother has always got to be going to Gimly School to talk to Teacher Joiner and get her boy out of trouble. I hear how you chase the girls and take popsies from the babies and tell your father such tales he'll not even listen to you anymore."

"He never listened, anyway," Raymond said and kicked at the wooden wheel of the pushcart. He would have gone and left old Gos, but he was drawn by the shiny, glinting figures of the noble Glom Gloom and the tiny Weeuns. All in different poses, each looked as if it had been suddenly turned to silver in the midst of life. He hadn't known Gos had such skill.

Here was Glom Gloom peering into the sunlight, a hand shading his eyes. So real that Raymond could almost see the squint of Glom Gloom's eyes under his hand. Here was a Weeun, crafty and wicked, its hands folded over its chest and its head tipped to one side as if it were sizing up Raymond in a most unpleasant way.

"They weren't fools, you know," Gos said, picking up the silver Tiny of the Weeun.

"I suppose you know that, too," Raymond said. "I don't believe there were ever any such things as Weeuns or Gartergates, or crooky-staffs, or even—" Raymond looked defiantly into Gos's eyes, "I don't even believe there was any Glom Gloom."

Gos looked calmly back at Raymond and said nothing. Raymond turned to leave, but his eye was caught by a Tiny lying apart from the other figures.

"What's this?" he asked. He picked up the Tiny, ex-

8

pecting Gos to hit him with the walking stick again. But Gos leaned on his pushcart and watched Raymond.

The silver Tiny showed a sheer mountain cliff. In the center of the cliff was a huge split, which looked as if a giant slice had been carved out of the stone. The split had been filled half way with blocks of stone that appeared to have been cut and laid up so precisely that not a crack would be left. The silver Tiny was so detailed that vines grew and twisted along the cliff and a minute cloud skittered across the sky above the scene.

"What is this?" Raymond asked again.

But it wasn't Gos who answered.

"It's the Gartergates, you fool. I don't suppose they teach you that in school anymore, do they?"

It was crazy old Wicker Bugle. She stood behind him, all thin bones, and her face webbed in lines and brown from being so much in the sun. She wore no holiday colors, just the same drab dress she always wore. Her gray hair was half pulled behind her head in a rough knot, half frizzed out like bramble bushes.

Raymond jerked his arm away from her outstretched hand.

"Don't touch me," he told her.

Wicker Bugle laughed. "Don't touch me," she mimicked, making her voice sound childish, afraid. She pulled her outstretched hand back and rubbed her palms together like a frightened old woman.

"I'm not afraid of you," Raymond said to her.

There was a quick exchange of looks between Gos and Wicker Bugle. Gos reached over and gently took the silver Tiny from Raymond's hand.

"And you shouldn't be afraid of her," he said. "She's no crazier than you or I."

Wicker Bugle threw back her head and laughed a loud, abandoned laugh. Her wide-open mouth showed gaps where her teeth were missing. A few Bulkings in the crowd turned and stared, then shook their heads.

"Now I'm not sure there's any sort of kindness in what you just told," she said to Gos, prodding him in the side with her elbow.

Gos smiled. "Could be you're right. Could be."

"What about the Gartergates? Are they for true?" Raymond asked impatiently, wishing they would remember just what was being discussed.

Wicker Bugle turned to him, the laughter suddenly gone from her eyes, her expression so fierce that Raymond took a step backward.

"Are they for true?" she said in a low angry voice, her face close to his. "Are they for true? Well you should ask. Everyone in Waterpushin should be asking that same question. They've all forgotten what Glom Gloom warned."

Wicker Bugle waved her hand angrily at the laughing, celebrating crowds. Her voice grew louder.

" 'But left to lie, prepare to die.' Oh, yes. They're for true, all right. But none of these fools even know what they look like. They've all forgotten. They have the memories of just-hatched wingers."

A small group of Bulkings stopped, watching and listening. Wicker Bugle was turning into another spectacle of Gloom Day.

"Fools! Simpletons! You're all doomed by your own ignorance! Your narrow-mindedness and soft ways will end you!"

Wicker Bugle went shouting into the crowds, waving her arms. Her long clothes flapped and fluttered around her skinny body like a dress drying on a windy day.

"Glom Gloom told you," she thundered. "And now remember the Gartergates. . . ."

She strode up to a Bulking man and pointed into his face.

"Do you know where the Gartergates are? Do you?"

The Bulking turned and walked away, saying, "Crazy old haggie."

For a moment Raymond thought that Wicker Bugle was going to follow after the Bulking. He felt a thrill of excitement at the thought of a fight.

"Is she going on again?" a tall Bulking asked.

"Pay no mind," someone else answered. "She's harmless."

Wicker Bugle suddenly let herself go quiet. The anger, the burning light in her eyes, slid away. Without it she seemed to shrink into a tired old woman.

The crowd of Bulkings wandered off, losing interest, already putting her out of their minds as they looked at more booths, more amusements.

Wicker Bugle turned and began walking away from Gos and Raymond. Her shoulders were hunched as if she were tired.

"Wait," Raymond called after her. "Where are the Gartergates? Tell me that, if they're for true."

But Wicker Bugle kept on walking as if she hadn't heard him.

Gos put his hand on Raymond's shoulder. "She won't be telling you that, even if she does know," he said.

Raymond shrugged off Gos's hand. "Then they're not for true? How did you make the Tiny, then?"

"I can't say they're for true and I can't say they're not." He nodded his head in the direction Wicker Bugle had gone. "*She* says they are. That's all I know. As to how I

11

made the Tiny, I did it the way she told me. She can talk in poetry when she's of a mind."

Raymond pushed his black hair away from his face.

"I should have known none of it was for true," he said. "Nothing but old stories."

"Who knows what's for true once a time is past? There's no way to prove how something was that's gone." Gos unhooked the little lever that kept the pushcart from rolling away. "And if a time is gone, what does it matter? It's all rain into rivers now."

Gos put his walking stick on top of his pushcart. "Good Gloom to you, Raymond. Mind your mouseling tail now."

Leaning against the bar of his pushcart, Gos pushed it down the Mid-cobbie, sing-songing as he went, "Fine Tinies. Make way for fine silver Tinies."

What *did* it matter? Gos was right. What's past was past. Knowing whether Glom Gloom or the Gartergates were for true wouldn't change anything now. Waterpushin life would go on just the same whether there were Gartergates or not.

In the square there was another performance of the stick figure show. Wicker Bugle was sitting with a group of children who were laughing at a stick figure Weeun. The Weeun was trying to hide behind a tree, but the tree kept walking away, leaving the Weeun exposed on the stage. The children shrieked with laughter each time the tree moved, but Raymond could hear Wicker Bugle's laughter above the children's.

There was no understanding the ways of Wicker Bugle. A little while earlier, she probably would have torn down the stage and smashed the stick figures in her rage at the ignorant Bulkings of Waterpushin.

2 · The Silver Tiny

GLOOM DAY was spoiled. None of it was for true. It was all just an excuse to go cavorting in the Mid-cobbie. A time for the Bulkings to be lazy and laughing for a day. A time when the shopkeepers and merchants could make extra pennies. When the children could run wild in the cobbies and wynds, happy to be free of their parents and their parents happy to be free of them.

Glom Gloom and the Weeuns were probably invented by some old Bulking, some wrinkled, wizened old Bulking who had nothing to do on a cold eve but spin his mind.

Raymond headed for home, leaving the holiday voices echoing between the houses of the village. The further he was from the Mid-cobbie, the more foolish the voices sounded.

His house was on the edge of Waterpushin, on a mean little wynd that twisted and turned away and around Waterpushin as if it were lost. There were holes and puddles in the wynd, which Raymond had to walk around or through. Usually he walked through them.

Hardly anyone ever came as far as his house, so Raymond walked unconcernedly along the middle of the wynd. He had a kind of swagger to his walk: a roll of each hip as he stepped, matched by a swinging of his shoulders. He had learned the swagger by watching the Fish Barrelers.

Raymond had once not gone to school for three days so he could watch the Fish Barrelers. Each morning at about the same time Teacher Joiner was ringing the school bell, Raymond would climb to the top of a stack of crates beside the dock where the Fish Barrelers worked. He stayed there all day, lying on his stomach and watching the Bulkings below him.

The Fish Barrelers stood in a line along the dock, from the boat they were unloading to the empty wooden barrels they filled at the other end of the dock. The Fish Barrelers in the boat would throw a fish up to the first Fish Barreler in the line. He would throw it to the next Fish Barreler and on up the line until all the fish were packed in the barrels and ready to be loaded onto the carts for market.

As the Fish Barrelers caught the fat, shiny fish, they shouted and sang bawdy songs and told stories about each other and their friends and the adventures they'd had. Raymond learned about grown-up, Bulking man things, about chewing bacco leaves and tossing games and other things he wasn't quite sure he understood.

But after three days Teacher Joiner met Raymond's mother on the Mid-cobbie and asked her what illness Raymond had and would he be well enough to come to school the next day.

Raymond's punishment had been to stay in his room every day after school for a week. His mother had cried because he was in trouble again, and his father had scowled angrily, not speaking. Teacher Joiner had made him do all the schoolwork he'd missed twice over.

"Are you enjoying Gloom Day?" Raymond's mother asked as he slammed the door into the kitchen. She was

14

cutting up paturnies and dropping them into a steaming pot on the stove. Her red and yellow cloak was lying over a chair by the table.

"There's no sense in it," Raymond said and kept walking toward his room.

"Raymond, mine," she said to him, but was only answered by the slamming of his bedroom door.

Dida Fibbey sighed and called out, "Raymond, I'm going to Gloom Day now."

There was no answer from behind Raymond's closed door, and Dida Fibbey sighed again but continued, "I'll be back before dinner hour."

There was still no answer, and Dida left the house, wishing she could understand her only child.

Raymond was lying on his bed in his tiny room. He often didn't answer when he was spoken to. It seemed easier somehow.

The ceiling of the little low cottage sloped down above his head so that if he didn't bend over before he got in and out of bed, he'd bump his head. There was only enough room to walk between his bed and the too-small wardrobe he'd had since he was born. But even so Raymond had managed to get into the room things that would have crowded a bedroom three times the size. His possessions were piled everywhere there was a flat space. Bird nests and old bones. Balls of string. Rocks. Pictures and books he'd had since he was a baby. Empty boxes and old bottles.

Nailed to the wall was a cap he'd taken off the head of Teacher Joiner one day on a dare, when Teacher Joiner had dozed in the school yard under a tree. Teacher Joiner had been furious, but no one dared tell him who had taken it because they were more afraid of Raymond than they were of Teacher Joiner. There were long, soft feathers from a huge red bird Raymond had found dead on the bank of the Waterpush River.

Raymond kept adding to the piles and stacks, and sometimes he'd take them apart to look down at the bottom and discover things he'd forgotten he had. But he never threw anything away. His mother had long since given up trying to clean his room.

Raymond looked up at his rough ceiling and thought about the old story of Glom Gloom. He was supposed to have memorized it in school, but he never had, except for the lines about the Finders mysteriously conquering the Weeuns and the last few lines about the Gartergates, because they were the most exciting parts.

When he'd believed the story of Glom Gloom was for true, he had often daydreamed that he was one of Glom Gloom's men. Loyal and brave. He'd imagined himself by Glom Gloom's side: always prepared to do as Glom Gloom bid; depended upon and trusted.

The old story said that once the Bulkings had lived in the Wideland, a huge island surrounded by the Bluey Seas. One day, the Weeuns, a strange, tiny but powerful people, had come from the Bluey Seas and hypnotized the Bulkings into becoming their slaves. The enslaved Bulkings had lived for seasons and seasons under the rule of the Weeuns. Then when Glom Gloom discovered a way to escape the hypnotism, he and a few loyal friends defeated the Weeuns. How, no Bulking now alive knew.

The Finders then led the Bulkings far, far into the Green Mountains to Waterpushin, a hidden land discovered by Glom Gloom, the great Finder. According to the old stories, the Finders built the Gartergates to insure forever that Waterpushin and the Bulkings would be safe from the Weeuns.

16

The village was called Waterpushin and the whole land was called Waterpushin, as if each were the other, and they both were the same.

Raymond didn't know of any Bulking who had ever been outside Waterpushin. There was no reason to want to go outside. He himself had only been as far as the edge of the Wild Hills. He tried to recall the map of Waterpushin that hung on the wall of his classroom in Gimly School, but he'd never paid close attention to it, even when it was being taught by Teacher Joiner.

There were the Green Mountains toward the rising sun, and the wide, angry Waterpush River toward the setting sun. The Waterpush came out of the Wild Hills as if it were being pushed. It crashed and boiled down into the valley, where it suddenly widened and smoothed, curving around the village of Waterpushin like a great, tame snake. The docks were on one shore of the Waterpush and a steep unclimbable cliff on the other. In this tame section of the Waterpush, the fishermen launched their boats and caught the fish the Bulkings ate.

Just past the village, the Waterpush seemed to suddenly remember it was a dangerous, angry river, and it roared away over huge boulders and rocky falls. Where it went after it passed to the edge of the Green Mountains, Raymond didn't know. If any Bulking had traveled the Waterpush River past the Green Mountains and lived, he'd never returned to Waterpushin to tell of it.

AT THE DINNER hour Raymond's mother excitedly talked of Gloom Day.

"It took me longer to see every booth this year than it ever has. I think this is the best Gloom Day ever."

She turned to Raymond. "Did you see the Gloom Cake booth? Such clever figures. That woman has such talent with her sugar frosting. I almost bought one to bring home to you."

"Mmmm," Raymond mumbled, and bent over his dinner, thinking of the sweet Gloom Cake dough and how it had tasted as he licked it from his fingers.

There were new red ear baubles dangling from Dida's ears, and she tossed her head in little dips and jerks so the swinging glowstones twinkled back the evening light.

Loper Fibbey sat at his end of the wooden table and silently ate his dinner. Gloom Day or not, he had worked all day painting the Majester's new house, and he was tired.

Majester Trader's new house was being built on a hill at the very edge of Waterpushin. There were no other houses on the hill, and already the Bulkings were calling the hill, "Majester's Hill." The new house looked down over the village, and as the Majester's wife said, "It has a commanding view of the Waterpush."

Some Bulkings said the Majester had chosen that spot for the new house because it would be the first house in Waterpushin to be touched by the morning sunlight and the last to lose the sunlight in the evening, the closest the Majester would ever come to wearing a golden crown.

Other Bulkings couldn't see what was wrong with the old Majester's house in the square. It had been good enough for every other Majester Waterpushin had ever had.

Dida suddenly clapped her hands together and stood up.

"Oh! I nearly forgot, Raymond. I have something for you."

She hurried to her cloak hanging on a peg beside the door and removed a small package wrapped in the page of a newspaper.

"That woman nearly scared me to tears when she came running up behind me and threw this at me. 'Give it to the boy,' she said and ran off again."

Dida handed the package to Raymond. "She certainly can move fast for an old woman."

"Who?" Raymond's father asked.

"Why, Wicker Bugle, of course," Dida said. "Who else in Waterpushin would act so odd?"

Raymond pushed his bowl aside and unwrapped the page of newspaper.

It was the silver Tiny of the Gartergates. It looked more delicate and fine than it had on Gos's pushcart. He stared down at the perfect vines along the stones. It almost seemed as if there were berries growing on them. He hadn't noticed before that there was a tiny flock of geese winging across the sky under the tiny cloud. They were in perfect formation, their wings all poised at the upstroke.

"Let me see that," Raymond's father said, holding out his hand.

Raymond pulled the Tiny against his chest.

"She gave it to me. It's mine." He stood up from the table and headed toward his bedroom.

"No crazy old haggie is going to be giving my son presents," Loper Fibbey said as Raymond closed his bedroom door.

Raymond heard the soft murmur of his mother's answer. He made out the word, "harmless."

He sat on his bed and touched the smoothness of the Tiny, wondering at Gos's precise workmanship. But as he held the small scene in his hands, he felt a roughness on the back of it. He turned it over, and there on the smooth back, scratched with something as pointed as a nail, were the unsteady words: FOR TRUE.

3 · Gimly School

T HE DAY after Gloom Day was like any other day in Waterpushin. The greatest Bulking holiday of the season was over. Holiday cloaks and dresses and arm bands were hung back in their places until the next holiday.

The Tidy Crews had cleaned the cobbies and wynds before anyone else was awake. The booths and streamers were gone. The stones in the square shone as bright and clean as if they'd been polished. Not even a red and yellow popsie wrapper was left lying in the Mid-cobbie.

In his bedroom, Raymond hurriedly dressed for school. He pulled a tunic with patched elbows over his head and buttoned a pair of pants with knees so thin he could feel the breezes when he ran.

After he tied his cloth boots he gently lifted the silver Tiny of the Gartergates from the top of his dresser. It seemed to glow. Raymond touched the raised little cloud with his fingertip and then polished his fingerprint away with the sleeve of his tunic. When he turned the Tiny over, the scratched words: FOR TRUE, shone up at him, rough and unsteady, like a child's printing.

Why had Wicker Bugle sent it to him? Did she really know that the Gartergates were for true? Raymond carefully wrapped the Tiny in a nose cloth and pushed it securely to the bottom of his pocket.

There were only three days of school left before the Warm Days began. Already, long before he woke in the mornings, Raymond's room filled with light from the tiny window by his bed. And at night it was still light outside when he fell asleep.

Warm Days. No more school. No more Teacher Joiner. He could forget about the school books and spend his time fishing and exploring along the banks of the Waterpush. If he were very careful, he could even slip away and do some forbidden hunting at the edge of the Wild Hills.

Between spoonfuls of porridge, Raymond asked his mother, "What do you think of the Gartergates?"

Dida Fibbey paused in surprise over the breakfast dishes she was stacking.

"The Gartergates? Why, I rarely think of them." She frowned as if trying to remember. "But if they're for true they must be doing their job. We certainly don't have any Weeuns in Waterpushin."

"Don't you think they're for true?" Raymond asked.

Until yesterday he had always believed in the legend of Glom Gloom and the Gartergates, and he had thought everyone else must believe in the old stories too.

Dida turned to her son, wiping her hands on a dish towel.

"It's not exactly that I don't believe they're for true," she said. "I believe it is an old story, and old stories always have some truth in them. But after seasons and seasons the stories become greater and greater and more exciting, until some parts are forgotten while other parts, mainly the adventures, are told and retold until they're remembered better than when they happened."

"But what about the Gartergates? Do you think that they're only an old story?"

Dida looked above Raymond's head, thinking long and carefully before she answered.

"I believe," she began, "that the Gartergates were once real, that perhaps they were a bridge or a wall to hold back water, something that was useful to Waterpushin when they were built. But that was a long, long time ago. There is no one who remembers anyone who remembers."

"Then you don't think the Weeuns were real either?"

"Wherever would they have lived?"

"On the outside, like in the old stories," Raymond suggested. "On the other side of the Gartergates?"

Dida looked at Raymond, frowning. "Outside," she mused. "There is no outside."

* * *

IT WAS a longish walk from Raymond's house to Gimly School. By the time Raymond had paused to look about the empty square, the cobbies were filling with Bulking children on their way to school.

Raymond walked alone, not looking at anyone else. He stopped to pick up a rock and throw it against a tree.

Thwunk! came back the satisfying sound as it hit the tree trunk squarely.

No one said hello to Raymond, and he kept his eyes from meeting anyone else's. He knew some of the students were afraid of him. There were times, not many, when he was sorry he didn't have more friends. But usually it was easier to be alone.

Bort Gard was standing under the tree at the corner of

23

Gimly School. Raymond walked past him, pretending he didn't see him.

"Hello, Raymond," Bort said and fell into step beside Raymond.

Raymond didn't answer. Bort always seemed to be around wherever Raymond went. Even when Raymond sneaked away with his slinger to hunt rabbits by the Wild Hills, Bort would sometimes materialize and tag along after him.

Bort was the same age as Raymond, but he was small, just like all the Gards. Bort's father was smaller than Raymond, and Raymond wasn't even at full growth.

The Gards were the best net menders in Waterpushin. All day long Bort's father and Bort's brother, Jerem, worked by the Waterpush, mending the torn nets of the fishermen with swift, graceful movements. Someday Bort would work all day with them, too.

All the Gards were skinny. Bort was even skinnier than skinny. His elbows stood out from his arms like tree nuts, and his knees were the widest part of his legs. He had skinny yellow hair and a skinny face. But his eyes were wide and round.

More than once when Raymond had been out slinging rabbits, Bort had pointed out the hiding place of a rabbit in the gray-green brush. If Raymond let the rock in his slinger fly at exactly the spot Bort said, either a rabbit would come bounding out, or, on inspection, he would find the still-warm body.

It was not the Bulking way to kill animals. The gray rabbits were always getting into the rich gardens, eating the produce just before it was ready to harvest. But the Bulkings didn't harm the rabbits; they patiently chased them away again and again.

The slinger was a secret. Raymond had made it himself from a piece of branch and a stretchy strap his father used to hold his paint brushes together.

There would be trouble if anyone discovered that Raymond hunted rabbits, even though the rabbits caused so much damage.

Raymond was used to trouble, but he knew Bort wasn't. Bort was never in trouble. Always clean, always polite.

Bort turned his head away when Raymond let his slinger go at a rabbit. But still he continued to appear when Raymond went hunting. It was Bort's own business if he wanted to risk trouble.

Raymond walked up the steps into Gimly School. He felt Bort just behind, like a skinny shadow.

There were two classrooms in Gimly School, across the hall from each other, one for the little graders, one for the bigger graders. Just inside the school door was a cloakroom where the students left their coats and lunches.

Teacher Joiner was standing by the door of the cloakroom, his finger pointed at one of the little graders, who was standing forlornly with mud on his face and a long tear across his tunic.

"What *will* your mother say," he asked, shaking his head.

Raymond stepped behind Teacher Joiner and pointed and shook his finger in imitation. Then he shook his head and crossed his eyes and pulled down the corners of his mouth.

The eyes of the little grader widened, and someone in the hall tittered and another bigger grader laughed out loud.

Teacher Joiner whirled around, but Raymond quickly relaxed his face and said, "Good morning, sir."

Teacher Joiner knew something had happened at his expense, but he didn't know what. Trust Raymond Fibbey to be at the bottom of it. He clapped his hands together angrily and said, "Everyone to their classrooms. At once."

The last bell hadn't rung yet, but the hall became quiet as the students hurried to their rooms.

Raymond tossed his lunch sack onto a shelf in the cloakroom and waited there until Teacher Joiner had entered the bigger graders' classroom.

Everyone was quietly seated, and Teacher Joiner was standing at the front of the room when Raymond entered, sauntering in his best Fish Barreler's walk. Teacher Joiner pursed his lips and watched Raymond seat himself but said nothing.

Bort turned from his seat across from Raymond and winked. Raymond looked away.

The bell rang.

"Spellers, everyone," Teacher Joiner said sternly, and the day began.

Throughout the morning Raymond glanced at the map of Waterpushin that hung on the wall by the door. The delicately colored map was set into a frame with a plate of glass over it for protection. The morning light reflected off the glass, and Raymond had to squint to see it.

He had hidden a piece of paper under his notebook, and he tried to copy what he could see of the map. But his proportions seemed all wrong. Once he saw Bort watching him with a puzzled expression. Raymond scowled at Bort until he turned back to his schoolwork.

There were only two maps of Waterpushin in the village: one in the Majester's house and one in Gimly School. Who needed a map of Waterpushin? All the Bulkings, even the smallest children, knew their way about Waterpushin.

Raymond wouldn't dare stand and study the map during recess or Teacher Joiner would become suspicious. And it seemed there was no way to copy the map. He looked at his crooked, childish drawing of Waterpushin and crumpled it in frustration. He would have to get a copy of the map for his own.

4 · The Map

RAYMOND SOFTLY opened the door to the Gimly School's gardening shed. It was an old door, and it creaked on its hinges as he pulled it.

The creak of the door seemed like a scream to his ears, but no lights went on. No door slammed in awakening alarm. Everything was as quiet as when he'd run from shadow to shadow from his house to Gimly School. The nearest lights were those at Merrily Cumbers's house, two doors down the cobbie from the school.

He felt along the wall inside the shed where he knew there hung an extra key to the school. It was supposed to be a secret that the key hung there, but he had seen Teacher Joiner take it once when he'd forgotten his own.

Raymond's hand brushed against a delicate spider web and scraped over the sharp point of a nail before he felt the solid metal of the key just above the height of his head. He slipped the key into his pocket as quickly as if someone might be watching him with eyes that could see in the dark.

Raymond had barely waited until his parents went to bed before he'd quietly left the house. There were a few houses with light showing from golden squares of window, but he'd only seen Bulkings on the cobbies once. Three men talking earnestly together. Stepping into a side cobbie, Raymond had watched them pass him unknowingly. Bulkings did not often go out by darkness.

Standing outside the shed and breathing deeply, he turned the key over and over inside his pocket. In the moonlight only a few stars were shining, and Raymond recognized the bright Singing Turtle constellation, the only constellation he knew. He'd heard the Fish Barrelers cursing, "by the tail of the Singing Turtle."

The tail of the Singing Turtle stars pointed directly down to where the Waterpush crashed away over the rocks, amid the cliffs no one had explored in Bulking memory.

He had to hurry. Already his mother might have gotten out of bed and, for some motherish reason, checked his room and found him missing. Or perhaps the lights were on in Merrily Cumbers's house because her father couldn't sleep and was getting ready to walk about his gardens.

Raymond took another deep breath and carefully walked around the building toward the broad front door of Gimly School. He wished there were a key to the back door. The front door faced directly onto the cobbie.

He tripped over a rock in the shadows and bit his lips to keep from gasping aloud.

The distance from the gardening shed to the front door of Gimly School had never seemed so long.

The key slid easily into the lock, and the door was open. He hadn't expected it to be so simple.

He'd never been in Gimly School when it was empty. It hung hollow and unknown around him. It was an echoing shell, filled with unfamiliar shadows and dark corners where anything might be hiding.

Raymond remembered the Fish Barrelers' song:

> *There's no fear in us.*
> *We've taken the test,*
> *And unlike the rest,*
> *We've turned out to be best.*

The Fish Barrelers had sung the song in a kind of pounding rhythm as they passed the fish up the line, from one to the other.

He squared his shoulders and walked rapidly down the hall, past the cloakroom to the door of his own classroom.

This door didn't squeak. It swung into the classroom as easily as if someone on the other side were pulling it open.

Shafts of moonlight showed in the tall windows, casting long shadows onto the floor from the desks. Teacher Joiner's desk loomed darkly, watching as sternly as Teacher Joiner himself watched during the day.

It was like a dream. Raymond wouldn't have been surprised if suddenly the school were to be filled with noisy children and bright daylight. Gimly School in darkness didn't seem real.

The map hung on the wall beside the door, its glass glowing dully.

Raymond touched the cool glass. This was the worst trouble he could be in. No one could help him if he were caught. Yet he *had* to know if the Gartergates were for true, if Wicker Bugle lied, or if the old stories lied.

Raymond lifted the map from the wall and set it on the floor. He felt along the back for the tacks that held it in the frame. They were pushed in loosely, and he was able to pry them out with his fingers. With the map face down on the floor in front of him, he felt carefully around the edges of the wooden backing, sliding his fingers until he finally could get a grip and pull up the wood, leaving only the map against the glass frame.

The map clung to the glass, but Raymond gently slid it off and rolled it into a long tube. Then he tied it with a piece of string he'd brought in his pocket. He put the wooden backing against the glass and pushed the tacks back in with his fingers. When he was finished, he lifted the empty frame and hung it in its place on the wall beside the door.

Taking the precious map, he left his classroom. Around him the empty school loomed, disapproving in its silence.

It was too much. He ran down the hallway, his feet echoing like thunder. The dark night was welcome after the eerie school. Raymond locked the door and quickly replaced the key in the shed.

He ran all the way home through the moonlit night, holding the map tightly under his arm.

5 · Teacher Joiner's Anger

*T*EACHER JOINER stood in front of the class with his hands on his hips. His face was red and his eyes darted about the room, stopping at one Bulking child, then moving on to the next.

No one moved. Not even Raymond had ever seen Teacher Joiner so angry. He looked as if he were about to burst. Behind him, leaning against the neat stack of books on his desk, was the empty frame of the map of Waterpushin. The blank glass gaped out at the silent classroom.

"Who knows anything about this?" Teacher Joiner demanded, pointing to the empty frame behind him but keeping his eyes on the students in the classroom.

Raymond sat as still as everyone else. His hands were folded on his desk and his eyes were solemnly on Teacher Joiner's red face. No one answered.

"I want to know who did this," he thundered, pointing again at the empty frame. "I'm convinced one of you must know how or why this happened."

Not a finger twitched or a shoulder shrugged. There was scarcely any breathing.

Raymond felt that Teacher Joiner's eyes rested a while longer on him than on anyone else, but he didn't move, not even to blink. He felt a shaking inside, a twitching around his mouth.

Finally Teacher Joiner gave a deep sigh.

"I see you either won't, or can't, tell me anything about this, this . . . theft. Nothing like this has ever happened in Gimly School, or even in Waterpushin." Teacher Joiner paused and then finished, "This is a terrible crime."

He turned and placed the empty frame on the floor in the corner behind his desk. For a few long moments he stood with his back to the classroom. Raymond took the chance to glance around him.

Eyes were wide and faces were white in contemplation of the theft. Everyone was watching Teacher Joiner and the empty map frame. It *was* a terrible crime. Bulkings rarely locked the doors of their homes, and shopkeepers weren't afraid to leave their shops unattended while they stepped out for a moment.

Raymond hadn't thought of taking the map as a *crime*. He only wanted to look for the Gartergates. Then he planned to return it.

"Now," Teacher Joiner said, turning back to face the room and brushing his hands together as if they were dusty, "let's get on with our lessons. Figures, please."

There was a sound like a breeze as the students let out the breaths they'd been holding and gratefully turned to their arithmetic lessons. From his desk, Raymond pulled a crumpled piece of paper that had yesterday's sums on it. As he straightened, his eyes met the eyes of Merrily Cumbers, who sat two seats across from him. She was looking directly at him with one eyebrow raised.

Raymond felt a sudden catch as he thought of the lights on in her house the night before. She couldn't have seen him. But she was looking at him as if she knew something secret. What else was there to know? He scowled at her, but she looked at him boldly, her eyebrow still raised as if she were waiting for a sign from him.

33

Merrily Cumbers had a way of meeting things head on. She was always the first to raise her hand and ask Teacher Joiner to explain what he meant. She was always asking, "Why?" Many times Raymond had watched Teacher Joiner call on someone in the class who wasn't prepared rather than acknowledge Merrily's waving hand. And she wasn't only that way in class. Raymond saw her running the girls' games in the school yard, always the one trying to tell everyone else what to do.

He turned his eyes from Merrily and studied his sums, determined not to look at her again. But he thought he felt her eyes on him several times during the morning.

"Going to play Whip-tag?" a voice asked as everyone rushed into the school yard for the lunch period.

Raymond looked behind him, knowing already he would see the dark face of Gillus.

Gillus lived with Gos, the pot-mender. He wasn't Gos's son. Everyone knew the story of how Gos had taken Gillus in after Gillus's father disappeared in a boat trip down the Waterpush, following the tail of the Singing Turtle, some said. Gillus's mother had died when he was still a baby, and she had been Gos's sister.

Gos and Gillus lived on a topsy-turvy houseboat not far from the Fish Barrelers' dock. The houseboat never went anywhere. It stayed tied to its own rickety dock and became more and more tumbledown every season. Gos had his workshop aboard the houseboat. From early morning until late at night, smoke rose from a forge Gos kept fired for his pot-mending and metal work.

"Not today," Raymond answered Gillus.

Gillus shrugged and headed for the grassy area where some of the other boys were already forming up sides for Whip-tag.

Gillus was the only student in Gimly School who made Raymond take caution.

"I'll be a leader," Gillus said loudly to the group getting ready to play Whip-tag.

No one argued with him.

Raymond took his lunch to a tree near the edge of the school yard. Three little grader girls were giggling under it, but when they saw Raymond walking toward them they scattered like frightened tweak-birds.

There were knots of children here and there in the playground, talking earnestly together. Guessing about the missing map, Raymond thought.

He munched on honey bread and thought about the missing map. There was no way anyone would find it. He'd hidden it under his bed behind a box of skins shed by snakes.

He wouldn't have a chance to study the map until he was sure his parents were asleep tonight. And he wouldn't be able to follow it until Freeday, when the Warm Days began. Two more days! His neck prickled as he thought of following the map into the Wild Hills or even into the Green Mountains. What other Bulking had been there, in any memory?

"Hello, Raymond."

It was Bort, standing just outside the shade of the tree and looking eagerly on. He was so skinny his clothes hung as unwrinkled as if they were still on a hanger.

"Bort," Raymond said and put the last piece of honey bread into his mouth. He chewed hard and tried to appear too busy to speak.

"Who do you think took the map?" Bort asked.

Raymond looked quickly at Bort's face, but Bort seemed to be asking an innocent question.

"How should I know?" he answered. "What good would an old map like that be to anyone? Every Bulking knows his way around Waterpushin."

"My father said the map was valuable as a part of our history because there are only two of them."

"How did your father know the map was taken?"

Bort hunkered down next to Raymond.

"Teacher Joiner called Constable Dragit this morning as soon as he discovered the map was gone. Constable Dragit saw my father outside and told him, and since I was still at home, my father told me."

Constable Dragit. So now he was involved, too. He was Waterpushin's only lawkeeper. Waterpushin was too peaceful to need more than one lawkeeper, and mostly what he did was to be sure Waterpushin was in order, that the lamps were lit at night and the cobbies were kept clean.

"So why did they put such a valuable map in Gimly School?" he asked Bort.

Bort frowned. "I don't know. It was long ago . . . before our fathers went to Gimly School. The maps could be showing the way *to* something." Bort's voice ended as if he were asking a question. "Do you think someone needs the map to find an old secret?"

"What do you mean? What secret?" Raymond asked angrily. If Bort could guess why the map was taken, then Constable Dragit might do the same!

Bort hastily stood up, backing away from Raymond's sudden anger.

"I . . . I don't know," he said uncertainly. "Maybe there's an old treasure somewhere? Maybe hidden at the Gartergates?"

"Do *you* think the Gartergates are for true?" Raymond asked.

36

Bort looked off toward the Green Mountains, which showed hazily above the treetops.

"I don't know," he said softly. "Sometimes I think they have to be for true. Otherwise why would there be such old stories and warnings? But other times I think they were just made up, for a good story."

The line of boys playing Whip-tag raced past, and suddenly Bort was flung headlong onto the ground like a gangly-jointed puppet. Raymond was certain he'd seen Gillus stretch out his arm and shove Bort.

When Bort picked himself up, there was a grass stain on one arm of his tunic and a tear in the knee of his pants. He brushed at himself, keeping his head down so Raymond couldn't see his face.

"Whip-tag can be rough," Raymond said.

Bort still didn't look up. "It depends on who's playing," he said and turned away.

Raymond watched him walk toward the school, his small thin body held tightly, grass still stuck to the back of his pants. Just as Bort reached the corner of the school, one of the girls playing skipping rope dropped out of line and ran after him. When she reached him, she put her hand on his arm and began to talk quietly to him. It was Merrily Cumbers.

6 · Merrily Cumbers

FTER LUNCH, Teacher Joiner was standing sternly in front of his desk as they all filed back into the classroom.

"I want you to know," he said when everyone was sitting silently and expectantly in their places, "that the Majester has authorized Constable Dragit to organize a Search and Find team to investigate the theft of the precious map of Waterpushin."

A Search and Find team. The last time a Search and Find team had been organized was when Dacey Stander was lost and feared drowned in the Waterpush. The Search and Find team had found him asleep under a tree in Majester Trader's back garden. Raymond had been a little grader when that happened.

"There will be no clue left idle," Teacher Joiner said. "If any of you know anything, any little thing at all, now is the time to come forward. We must have the return of our map. It belongs to all of us."

Raymond thought of the rolled map lying under his bed and wished he had hidden it more carefully. By now the news must be all over Waterpushin that one of the two old maps had disappeared. He willed the hours of the school day to go as rapidly as possible so he could find a better hiding place. There would be no chance of returning the map until the excitement settled.

38

When the long school day was finally over, Raymond ran from the classroom.

Little graders and bigger graders filled the hall, their voices high in relief that the day was finished.

"Toss me my lunch sack," someone said behind Raymond as he took his own from a shelf in the cloakroom. He ducked as a lunch sack flew over his head and was caught by another bigger grader.

He impatiently passed around a group of little graders on the steps. The afternoon sun was still high in the sky. It shimmered on the flat leaves of the trees and heated the stones of the cobbies.

Raymond was the first student out the school gate.

"Raymond Fibbey!"

It was Merrily Cumbers rushing after him, her long yellow hair bouncing around her face. She easily caught up with him and began walking in step beside him.

"What do you want?" Raymond asked her, lengthening his step.

"I want to talk to you."

"Well, I'm in a hurry. And asides, I don't want to talk to you," Raymond told her.

Raymond's long steps had taken him a few lengths past her when she said in a soft, lilting voice, "I know who took the map."

So she *had* been awake when he'd seen the lights in her house. Had she actually seen him, or was she just guessing? Raymond stopped, trying not to show the fear he was feeling.

"And how would you know?"

Merrily tossed her head so her hair fell away from her eyes.

"Oh, I know all right. And I think you know, too."

"How would I know, and why would I care who took a useless old map?"

"That's what I'm wondering."

Raymond shook his head and turned away from her. "I don't have time for any girls' foolishness. I'm going home."

Merrily ran after him and gripped his arm with both her hands. Raymond shook his arm. He shook it harder than he intended and Merrily reeled backwards, waving her arms desperately to keep her balance. It was no use.

She fell onto the cobbie on her bottom, gasping as she landed and her hair spilling over her face.

Behind them, students leaving Gimly School stopped and stared at Raymond and Merrily. None came forward to see what was happening.

Raymond looked down at the disheveled Merrily in shock. He hadn't meant to knock her down. A Bulking man *never* hurt a Bulking woman. He had been taught that from his earliest days. A Bulking woman was revered, no matter what her temperament. An argument between Bulkings was never resolved by laying hands on one another.

Merrily's face was blazing red as she scrambled to her feet and rushed at Raymond. She stopped so close to him he could feel her breath. Her eyes were wide and her hands in fists.

"You sneaky, lying toad. You're no better than a Weeun," she said in an angry, sputtering voice too low for the watching students to hear.

"You took that map. We saw you running from Gimly School last night." She shook her fist in Raymond's face. "And moreover, if you don't meet us under the Tailor Tree at the sixth bell tonight, I'll go directly to Teacher Joiner's house and tell him what I know."

Merrily turned and ran in the opposite direction, back

40

toward Gimly School and her house. Her feet in their soft shoes made no sound as she ran, but the students who were standing in front of the school watched her pass by as if she were clattering, stone on stone.

Raymond stared after her. What did she mean: "*We saw you,*" and, "meet *us?*" Who else had seen him? Was she telling the truth? Could she actually know he had taken the map?

All he'd wanted to do was look at the map. He'd never expected so much trouble, Now, getting the map back into the frame at school would be harder than taking it.

7 · The Meeting Under the Tailor Tree

HEN the Majester and his family can move in, and the party can still be Freeday eve?" Dida Fibbey asked her husband at dinner.

"Aye," said Loper Fibbey. "I've told them all along they needn't worry, that the new house would be finished on time. Even tomorrow, we'll begin moving things from the old house to Majester's Hill. They'll be sleeping snug inside the night before the party."

"Is it as beautiful inside as some have said, more beautiful than any home in Waterpushin?"

"It'll suit the Majester," Loper Fibbey said and refilled his bowl from the soup pot in the middle of the table.

Dida turned to Raymond, frowning. "Is that all you're going to eat?"

Raymond had only taken two spoonfuls of the thick soup, and his bread was untouched. The fifth bell had already rung on the little wall clock above the table, and his stomach was churning. Would Merrily actually tell if he didn't show up at the Tailor Tree by the sixth bell? He had a feeling she would.

"I'm not hungry," he told his mother.

"You're not feeling ill, are you?" she asked and placed her palm against Raymond's forehead.

Raymond pushed back his chair and stood so that her hand fell away from his forehead.

42

"I'm just not hungry, that's all."

"No fever." He heard her puzzled voice as he stepped out into the garden.

The garden was still and warm, the bright flowers drooping slightly in his mother's neat flower beds. Raymond stretched out on the grass under the tall yellow flowers his mother called "sun dials." They bent over him like a ceiling, their yellow petals casting shadows on the ground.

The map was still under his bed. He'd felt for it after school, afraid it would somehow be gone, but there it was, still rolled and tied, with a few dust balls clinging to the soft paper. He didn't dare take a look at it, not yet. He had to know what Merrily knew first.

Perhaps it was a trap. Merrily might have already told Constable Dragit, and he and his Search and Find team would be there, waiting under the Tailor Tree for Raymond. He still couldn't think who the other Bulking might be when she'd said, "*We* saw you."

If he didn't meet her, she was sure to tell. He had to believe that if he did meet her, there was a chance no one else would discover he was the thief who had taken the map.

The Tailor Tree stood halfway up the hill to the Majester's new house. No other tree in Waterpushin looked like the Tailor Tree. Its dark trunk was as big around as Raymond's room, and its thick branches and leaves spread out like a huge umbrella.

It was called the Tailor Tree because long ago an old tailor had set up shop under its shelter, hanging his clothes on the branches, and sticking his pins and threads and ribbons into the bark of the wide trunk. Raymond's mother had only been a little girl then, but the tree was still known as the Tailor Tree.

As Raymond approached the Tailor Tree, he thought he could make out two shapes under the shadowy branches, but no one else. He watched for movements that might mean Constable Dragit or members of the Search and Find team, but he saw nothing other than the two still shapes. Could someone be hiding behind the tree trunk? He walked in his best Fisher Barreler walk, determined not to let Merrily Cumbers see his fear.

A few lengths from the Tailor Tree one of the figures sitting in the deep shadows rose and came forward. It was Merrily. She blocked his view of the other shadowy Bulking, still sitting, unmoving, on the ground. There was a slight, uncertain smile on Merrily's face.

"I'm glad you came," she said to him. She wasn't speaking in the taunting way she had outside Gimly School. Maybe she really *didn't* want to tell Constable Dragit what she knew about the missing map.

"You didn't give me any choice, did you?" he retorted, trying to peer around her at the other figure.

Merrily gripped her hands together in front of her and looked down at them.

"It was the only way I could think . . ." she began.

Raymond stepped around her and walked deeper into the coolness under the dark branches, toward the other Bulking who sat with his arms wrapped around his knees.

He knew who it was. Without seeing the face, he recognized the skinny arms and legs, the bony elbows.

"Bort!"

His anger exploded, the horrible anger that got him into so much trouble and that other Bulkings didn't seem to share. It was like a hot fire inside his head, burning and flaring and sending him into doing angry actions before he could think.

44

He rushed toward the hunched, unmoving Bort, wanting to pound him, to make him hurt.

But Merrily jumped in front of Bort. Raymond stopped, shaking. His eyes squeezed shut as he tried to control himself, his body held stiff. He wouldn't hit Merrily. He couldn't.

"Get out of my way," he growled through teeth clenched so tight his jaws hurt.

Merrily put her hand on Raymond's arm.

"It's my fault, Raymond. He didn't want to be any part of it. I tricked him, just as I did you."

"And how did you do that?" he asked. If only she'd move out of his way.

"Sit down, Raymond, and listen to me," Merrily pleaded. She looked at him earnestly, her bright blue eyes piercing into his own.

"Is this another trick?" How could he believe her?

Merrily let go of his arm. She crossed her fingers over her chest in the childish "truth" sign.

"No tricks, I promise. Just the truth from now on." Merrily motioned to a place on the ground under the tree. "Please . . ."

Raymond glared at Bort, who still sat hunched, his eyes downcast and his knuckles white. Raymond shook his fist.

"You'd better tell me the truth, both of you."

He sat stiffly on the mossy ground, his back straight and his arms crossed, waiting. The branches of the Tailor Tree whispered together over their heads.

"My father tore his fishing nets yesterday on logs in the Waterpush," Merrily said, sitting on the ground between Bort and Raymond. "He needed help repairing the nets so he could fish this morning, and Bort's father sent

45

Bort over. It took a long time, but after the nets were
repaired I walked outside with Bort to see if the greenie flies
were out yet."

Raymond nodded. Everyone at Gimly School, and
probably half of Waterpushin, knew that both Merrily and
Bort loved crawlies and wingers, all those minute things that
most Bulkings paid no attention to until they buzzed around
their heads.

"We were standing by my gate talking when Bort said,
'What's that?' I couldn't see anything, but you know how
well Bort can see, and he said, 'Why, it's Raymond Fibbey
running with something under his arm.' Sometimes you do
rather . . . different things, so I didn't think much about it
until this morning at school when Teacher Joiner an-
nounced the missing map."

Merrily paused and shook her head in memory. "My,
wasn't he angry?"

Neither Raymond nor Bort replied.

"When I asked Bort to find out why you wanted the
map, he refused. So I told him that if he didn't go along
with me, I'd tell Constable Dragit what you'd done."

Merrily spread her hands toward Raymond, her palms
up. "So you see, Bort's here because he's your friend. He
didn't want me to tell."

"So what do YOU want?" Raymond asked her.

"I want to know why you took the map. I have a feeling
you're looking for an adventure, and I want to be part of it."

Raymond said a word he'd learned from the Fish Barrelers.

"What good could you be after you've proven you're a
sly trickster? How could I ever trust you?"

"You can trust us. We'll make a pact never to tell anyone, if you let us come with you."

Raymond looked over at Bort and felt his dampened anger rising again.

"I didn't think that you would try to trick me," he said to Bort.

Bort lifted his head. "I'm ashamed to be part of this deceit," he said.

Merrily angrily tossed her head.

"But you can trust me to be loyal." Bort looked at Merrily. "I won't say a word about the map, whether you decide to include us in your adventure or not."

Raymond nodded. He believed Bort, but as for Merrily . . .

"I didn't want to be deceitful, either," Merrily said, "but you never would have asked me to come along on your own."

"Who said I was going to ask you to come along as it is? What makes you think there's any adventure?"

Merrily sat quietly, looking down toward the village, and then she said, "Just once. Just one time I'd like to do something without a mother or a father or a teacher telling me what's right and what's wrong and how it should be done. Just once I'd like to do something they knew nothing about. Something that would belong to me, not them."

Bort looked from Merrily to Raymond, his head slightly nodding.

Just once. Something that belonged only to him. As long as Raymond could remember, he'd been fighting to do what he wanted. And what he wanted, more often than not, was against some Bulking way: either his parents' or Teacher Joiner's or the Majester's or some long-followed Bulking custom.

What Gos had said was true: trouble followed him like the tail of a mouseling. Not because he searched for trouble but because he wanted to know the "why" of things. Most Bulkings didn't want to be bothered with the "why." It was enough that there were old rules and old stories. It was easier to accept them as the "Bulking way" than to worry out their reasons and beginnings.

"All right. I'll tell you why I took the map."

Raymond told them about his doubts on Gloom Day, about crazy Wicker Bugle giving him Gos's Tiny of the Gartergates with the words, FOR TRUE, scratched on the back. And finally, about sneaking into Gimly School and taking the map to see if the Gartergates were there.

"And were they?" Merrily asked, her eyes bright with eagerness.

"I don't know," Raymond told her. "I haven't been able to look for them yet."

"What did you do with the map?" Bort asked.

Raymond hesitated. "It's well hidden."

Merrily chewed on a fingernail. Then she said firmly. "Let's go look at it."

"It's hidden," Raymond repeated.

"Can't you find it?" Merrily demanded.

"Of course I can, but I don't want to."

With her jaws tight Merrily said, "I think you'd better show us the map."

Raymond stared back at her angrily. What could he do? He jumped to his feet and began walking rapidly down the hill. He heard Merrily and Bort scrambling up from the ground behind him and running after him. He stretched out his pace. Let them hurry to keep up.

Raymond's mother was sitting in the kitchen mending one of Loper Fibbey's tunics when Raymond entered. Bort and Merrily were only a few lengths behind, their faces red from trying to keep up with Raymond.

"Raymond, where . . ." she began. When she saw Merrily and Bort, she set her sewing aside and stood up in surprise. Raymond never brought friends home with him.

"Why, hello, Merrily. Hello, Bort," she said.

Raymond walked past her toward his bedroom, leaving Merrily and Bort standing in the kitchen.

"Hello, Mrs Fibbey," Merrily said with her eye on Raymond's direction.

"Hello," Dida repeated. "How nice to see Raymond's friends. Would you like a sweetun or a glass of juice?"

"Thank you, Mrs. Fibbey," Merrily replied, "but I think we'll go visit with Raymond now."

"Of course," she said, waving her hand toward Raymond's room. "You go right along."

Raymond was sitting on his bed when Merrily and Bort entered.

They stood in the cramped room and looked around at the piles and stacks and boxes full of Raymond's treasures.

Merrily whistled through her teeth.

"Well. This is certainly a good place to hide the map," she said. "Nobody could find anything in here."

"You can leave whenever you want. I didn't invite you here."

Merrily looked contrite. "I'm sorry. That was rude of me." She picked up a shell and peered into it.

"This is very beautiful. It's wonderful that you save so many things. You can keep them near you and look at them whenever you want."

"Don't overdo it," Raymond said.

Merrily set the shell down and curtly asked, "Where's the map?"

"Not so loud," said Bort, glancing at Raymond's open bedroom door.

Raymond nodded. "Keep your voice down."

"Sorry!"

Raymond got up and closed the door. There was barely room for the three of them to stand in his bedroom. He motioned for Bort to sit on the end of the bed while he crawled under and retrieved the map.

"This is it," he said as he untied it.

He spread the map before them on his bed and weighted each corner, using clean pearly stones he'd found by the Waterpush. The map seemed more fragile, more luminous than it had when it was hanging in the schoolroom. The colors were more delicate and the lines finer. Every pen stroke was visible. Raymond touched it gently and felt the raised areas around the lines.

"It's lovely," said Merrily.

"What fine workmanship," added Bort. "I wonder why I never noticed it before."

"Because it was just part of the classroom," answered Merrily. "You never pay any attention to a part of school unless you have to."

"I guess you're right."

Raymond sighed impatiently. "Look for the Gartergates, will you?"

They bent their heads and traced their way around and around the map, each one going over what the other had already gone over.

Here was the Waterpush River, complete with tiny inked rapids where the Waterpush jumped out of the Wild Hills and frothed and pushed its way into the valley. Here were the Green Mountains, all steep and craggy to the east with a bright yellow sun rising sleepily over their impenetrable cliffs. Raymond slid his finger lightly over the delicate imitation of Waterpushin, touching the miniature buildings of the square, following the cobbies and wynds.

Double checking, triple checking, until the map became just a series of fine lines and muted colors. No sign of the Gartergates, not by name or drawing. No tiny inked stones to match the silver Tiny. Nothing that could even be taken as a symbol for the Gartergates.

Finally, Raymond sat back and said, "It's useless. The Gartergates aren't there. It must be just an old Bulking story."

"It looks so," Bort said and sat beside Raymond, leaning against a box of old toys.

Only a lovely old drawing of Waterpushin. For that he had chanced the anger of Teacher Joiner and who knew what other consequences if he were found out.

"Now I have to make a plan to return the map without getting caught. That will be harder than taking it."

Merrily still sat poring over the map.

"What artists they were who made these maps. I feel I could touch the leaves on these trees. And look, here's a tiny flock of geese flying under a cloud. They look as tiny as wingers, but I can almost see their feathers."

"Geese?" Raymond asked. "A flock of geese under a cloud? Are their wings all raised?"

Merrily turned to him. "Yes, all together. Did you notice them, too?"

"Let me see it," Raymond nearly shouted and got to his knees beside Merrily.

"Right here."

Merrily pointed to the flock of geese making their way across the sky under a puff of cloud. The entire scene was no larger than Raymond's thumbnail.

There was no mistaking it. The tiny scene was identical to the flock of geese winging their way across the silver Tiny that Wicker Bugle had given him.

"This is it!"

"What do you mean?" Merrily asked. "It's only a flock of geese."

"It's a clue," Raymond said and reached into his pocket for the silver Tiny. He pulled the sparkling Tiny out and held it up next to the map.

"Look! Here's the same flock of geese, the identical cloud. Gos and Wicker Bugle said it was a miniature of the Gartergates." He turned the Tiny over. "And here's where Wicker Bugle scratched FOR TRUE."

Merrily and Bort each looked at it, matching it against the scene on the map.

"You're right," Bort said. "Whoever made the map must have wanted to keep the Gartergates a secret."

"Why did they want them to be a secret if the old stories warn us to keep the Gartergates strong?" Merrily asked.

Bort tapped the Tiny. "But they left clues so the Bulkings would know where the Gartergates were.'

"And over the seasons," added Merrily, "the clues were lost, and the Bulkings forgot."

Raymond frowned. "But not lost to Wicker Bugle. Somehow, she knew."

The geese were flying over a spot where the Green Mountains began at the edge of the map. Raymond put his finger on the scene.

"If there *are* Gartergates, this must be where they are, right here under this flock of geese."

Raymond gazed longingly at the map as if it might reveal more secrets.

"I'm going on Freeday," he said.

Merrily held the Tiny up to the light from Raymond's tiny window. "We're all going on Freeday. We can meet under the Tailor Tree at the ninth bell in the morning."

Raymond and Bort exchanged a look of wariness.

Merrily saw it and said, "I'll bring sweetcakes, and I'll wear pants instead of a skirt. You'll see I can keep up with you."

"You'd better be able to," Raymond told her, "because if you can't and get lost, we won't have to worry about your telling anyone about the map, will we?"

8 · On Majester's Hill

ON FREEDAY, Raymond got up before his mother and father. He didn't want to risk his father giving him chores to do and keeping him from meeting Bort and Merrily.

He dressed quietly and pulled his cloth bag from under his bed. The night before he'd packed it with his slinger and some honey bread and sweetcakes taken from the kitchen. And before he went to bed, he'd carefully copied, on a clean sheet of paper, the portion of the map that showed the flock of geese winging across the sky and the edge of the village. That piece of paper was folded at the bottom of the bag, and the map was back under his bed. Now, he took the silver Tiny of the Gartergates from his pants pocket and slipped it into the bag, also.

Raymond closed the door to the house as softly as a whisper. He didn't let himself breathe freely until he was out of the gate. Then he slung the strap of his cloth bag over his shoulder and softly whistled to himself as he hurried along the wynd.

It was a good long while before he was to meet Merrily and Bort, but he wanted the time to himself, to think and plan.

The cobbies and wynds were empty. It was Freeday, a day on which no Bulkings got out of bed early unless they had to.

Or unless they were on an adventure, Raymond thought. And who did he know beside himself who went on adventures?

Raymond ran across the silent square, which would soon be filled with traders selling their wares, bustling and calling to each other and their customers.

But for now the square was empty; the shutters of the Majester's house were tightly closed. Majester Trader and his family had finished moving into the new house on Majester's Hill the day before, and tonight all of Water-pushin would gather on Majester's Hill to celebrate the new house.

"Where you be heading, Raymond?"

Raymond jumped in surprise. He hadn't seen Gillus stepping out from a side cobbie. He was holding a length of metal slightly behind his leg.

"Off to go fishing," Raymond lied easily. "Where you be heading?"

Gillus spit a long stream of bacco onto the cobbie.

"I'm collecting for Gos."

He held up the piece of metal. Raymond recognized it as a side brace from a wagon. "He has to have something to mend his pots and make the Tinies some Bulkings seem to like so well."

"Gos is talented," Raymond said noncommittally.

Gillus held his body and talked in the same manner as Gos. Even his expressions were like a young Gos.

"You'd better hurry on your way before all the rabbits go into hiding," Gillus said.

"I said I was going fishing."

Gillus looked carefully at Raymond's cloth bag. Raymond glanced down at the lump that was his slinger. He hoisted the bag higher on his shoulder so that its bulk shifted. Gillus spit another stream of bacco onto the cobbie.

"Maybe you don't know very much about fishing."

Raymond stood straighter and met Gillus's eyes.

"I fish my own way," he said.

Gillus shrugged and swung the length of metal idly, back and forth, back and forth.

"I'm sure you do. Don't lose yourself in the Wild Hills."

"*You* have no need to worry about me."

"And no want," Gillus said, waving the metal at Raymond. "Good fishing—or hunting." He crossed the cobbie, heading toward the Waterpush River and the houseboat he shared with Gos, humming the Fish Barrelers' song.

Raymond watched Gillus disappear. He had suspected for a long time that Gillus knew he hunted rabbits. And even though he'd never seen him in the Wild Hills, Raymond suspected that Gillus also did the forbidden hunting of the pesty rabbits.

By the time Raymond reached the mist-shrouded hillside, the magic of the morning was on him again. The grass was wet with dew, but the moss under the Tailor Tree was dry. He sat down on the springy green moss next to the trunk and looked down at the empty village.

Then he turned and looked behind him up the hill at Majester Trader's new house. Very proud and stately.

He felt as if he were totally alone, that nothing else existed, not Waterpushin, not even the old stories or the Gartergates. Just Raymond Fibbey and the Tailor Tree.

Sometimes he wished he *could* live by himself. If he truly lived alone, he could eat fish from the Waterpush and berries and wild plants from the Wild Hills. He could eat and sleep when he wanted, and play and hunt wherever he desired. He would be free, really free.

He didn't want to be a painter like his father, or a fisherman or a shopkeeper, not even a Fish Barreler. He wanted to explore, to be an adventurer like Glom Gloom and his men. But what was there left to explore in Water-pushin?

The sun finally came over the Green Mountains, and he realized that whoever had said it was right: the first thing the sun touched in the valley was the Majester's new house. The windows twinkled and sparkled as they reflected the golden light. The Majester probably *would* feel as if he were wearing a crown.

The morning was turning away from Raymond and becoming just another day, belonging to everyone.

He saw Merrily long before she began climbing the hill to the Tailor Tree. Her yellow hair, hanging in a tail down her back, shone brightly, and she was wearing some kind of green pants. There would be talk if any of the mothers saw *that*.

"Hello," she said, dropping herself and a large cloth bag down on the moss beside him. "Is Bort here yet?"

"Do you see him sitting here?"

Merrily looked around the shelter made by the Tailor Tree.

"No, I don't," she said, shaking her head. "Did you remember to bring the drawing of the map?"

Raymond didn't answer. She couldn't leave anything alone. Always bossing and trying to order everyone about.

"You're not at Gimly School with all the giggly girls," he said. "I'm the leader. I'm the one who will decide when and where we search for the Gartergates. Don't be ordering me about. Just leave everything to me."

Merrily pulled her long tail of yellow hair forward and rolled it between her hands.

"I'm the one who found the clue to the Gartergates on the map. Don't be forgetting *that*."

"*If* there really are Gartergates. We don't know that the flock of geese means anything. Don't forget, Wicker Bugle is the one who designed the Tiny—and you know what everyone says about her."

"Crazy old haggie," Merrily murmured.

They sat in silence, each of them thinking of Wicker Bugle.

She had once been very beautiful, Dida Fibbey had told Raymond, but always a little odd. She lived alone in a house at the edge of the Wild Hills. Very few Bulkings had ever seen Wicker Bugle's house. It was said to be made of dirt, little better than a hole in the ground.

Wicker Bugle had never had a husband or child, not even a pet that anyone knew. Just herself. Perhaps being alone so much was what had made her odd. She was always ranting and flapping her arms in the streets of Waterpushin, such a common sight that no one paid any attention.

"Bort's late," said Merrily. "Do you think we should go without him?"

"He'll be here. We'll wait."

"Constable Dragit came to our house last night and asked my father if he'd seen anything the night the map was taken," Merrily said.

"Had he?" Raymond asked.

"No," Merrily answered, pulling up bits of moss from the ground. "He asked me if I'd seen anything."

Raymond waited for her to continue, not wanting to let her know how her words frightened him.

"I told him I hadn't seen anything either," Merrily said. "And I didn't see anything. It was too dark." She shook her head. "I wasn't lying, not really."

58

"Here he comes," Raymond said, pointing down the hill.

Bort came from the south rather than up the path. He was running, darting first in one direction, then the other. His elbows pumped at his sides, and his cloth bag bumped against his legs.

"I wonder what's wrong," Merrily said.

Bort was a fast runner, and he was soon under the Tailor Tree, his face red, his breath coming in great gulps. He threw himself on the moss beside Merrily and Raymond.

"I'm . . . sorry I'm . . . late," he said. "My father . . ." He stopped to breathe deeply.

"What about your father?" Raymond demanded. "Does he know what we're doing?"

Bort shook his head and held up his hand, signaling Raymond to wait until he caught his breath.

Raymond watched Bort impatiently. At least his father didn't know.

"What happened?" Raymond asked.

"When my father went to the shed to get the wagon this morning, he discovered someone had taken it apart."

Raymond thought of Gillus and the metal side brace from a wagon he had been carrying.

"Father called Jerem and me into the shed to help put it back together," Bort told them.

"Did you get it back together?" Merrily asked.

Bort shook his head. "The side brace was gone. Everything else was there, but we couldn't put it together with the side brace missing. My father has never had such a thing done to him before. I sneaked away when he went to see Gos about having a new side brace made." Bort paused and looked down at the ground, frowning. "I may be in trouble when I get home."

Raymond wondered if Gos would sell Bort's father his own side brace.

"Are you sure you should come with us?" Merrily asked.

Bort nodded with certainty. "It will be worth any trouble," he said.

Raymond pulled the drawing of the map out of his cloth bag, unfolded it and smoothed it on his leg.

"This is where we are now," he said, pointing to an x he'd marked at the Tailor Tree. "And this is where we want to go," he finished, pointing to his sketch of the flock of geese.

"There must be an old path," Bort said.

"Wouldn't it be completely grown over and invisible by now?" Raymond asked.

"If the Gartergates are for true, and if they are as big as they appear on the Tiny that Wicker Bugle gave you, it must have taken many trips with rocks and mortar to build them. That much travel should have left a depression in the ground."

Merrily said thoughtfully, "We ought to go to a high point and look down at the area where the path might begin."

"I know!" she said and jumped up. "Let's go to the top of Majester's Hill! Bort should be able to see any path."

"I'll decide that," Raymond said sternly.

"That *is* a good idea," Bort said. "With my keen sight, Raymond . . ."

Raymond had a sudden feeling of shame. It *was* a good idea. He put the map in his pocket and held out his smaller bag to Merrily.

"It may be a long walk. Would you like to trade bags? Mine is lighter."

Merrily hesitated.

"Thank you," she said with a quick smile and handed her own bag to Raymond.

They passed around the Majester's new house, just out of sight of the windows. It wouldn't do to have the Majester see them and wonder what they were up to.

Preparations were beginning for that night's party. Four bakers in white jackets were carrying covered platters through the gates into the house, and delicious smells reached Bort and Merrily and Raymond as they hurried past.

Gos had made the fence and gate around the Majester's new house. Every Bulking had talked about it when it went up. The fence was made of long thin bars, spaced too close together for any Bulking to squeeze through. There were sharp points at the top of each bar. Never before had such a fence been built in Waterpushin.

"I can't wait to see inside," said Bort. "Has Trillia shown you?" he asked Merrily.

Trillia Trader and Merrily were good friends.

"No," said Merrily. "Trillia told me her father said the new house must be a surprise to everyone, even their friends." Merrily looked back at the straight lines and no-nonsense corners of the Majester's house. "My mother said the party tonight will be like a brag-party, a show-offy."

Behind the Majester's house, out of sight, they peered down the other side of the hill. Puffs of mist clung here and there to the trees in the shade of the Green Mountains.

"It's beautiful," Merrily said, smiling toward the mountains. "I've never been up here before. Isn't that strange? It's so close, but I've never come up here."

"Very few do," Bort said. "Most Bulkings have everything they want to see right in the village."

He shaded his eyes and looked into the distance to where the Green Mountains lowered themselves to the Waterpush.

"Can I look at the map, Raymond?" Bort asked.

Raymond unfolded the drawing of the map and held it out to Bort. Merrily and Raymond stood back and watched him, being still, trying not to break Bort's concentration.

Bort looked for a long time, occasionally glancing down at the map and shifting his gaze slightly. Raymond looked just as intently, trying to see where there might have once been a path or a trail through the woods, but he saw nothing, only a thick forest of varied trees that sloped upward toward the Green Mountains.

Suddenly Bort gasped, and his body began to tremble.

Merrily jumped forward and put her arm around his thin shoulders.

"What's wrong? Are you all right?"

Bort leaned forward, letting Merrily's arm support him. It was as if his whole body were trying to follow what his eyes saw.

"I see it," he said in a voice filled with awe. "I see a line through the forest with lower trees. It turns a little now and then like an old path. I never actually believed it was for true, but there it is. I wanted to believe it . . ."

Merrily put her other arm around Bort and laughed happily. Raymond turned away in embarrassment. Yet when he looked down, his own hands were trembling with excitement. He wouldn't believe it yet. It might just be a path made by animals. *He* couldn't see it. But he wanted to believe it was for true. He wanted to believe it more than anything.

9 · The Discovery

T FIRST neither Merrily nor Raymond could see any sign of an abandoned path. They followed Bort blindly into the tall forest, staying close to him, pausing when he paused to peer ahead or to the side. Bort studied the trees, his eyes traveling quickly over the branches and trunks and down to the forest floor.

Merrily and Raymond followed Bort's glances and tried to see what he was seeing, but it all looked the same: a meaningless forest of endless trees and plants. Merrily once caught Raymond's eye and shrugged her shoulders, rolling her eyes upward. In spite of himself, Raymond nodded in agreement.

Bort frequently stopped to set three stones on top of one another or to slash a piece of bark from a tree with his net-mending knife.

"So we can find our way out again," he explained to Merrily and Raymond.

But after a while Raymond began to feel where the path might be. It wasn't anything he could actually "see." It was more of an anticipation as to which direction they should turn next. Once he saw a pile of moss-covered stones. There was something unnatural about the tumbled stones, as if they might have been left aside to clear the path. Or maybe it was a cache of rocks left long ago to be used by future Bulkings?

The walking was easy. The forest was so old and the trees so tall that the ground was too shaded for bushy, brambly brush to grow. Only rich, green, hardy plants thrived here.

Finally the forest opened up into a small meadow. The three blinked in the warm sunlight. Behind them and on either side was the forest. Across the meadow was a steep cliff. The cliff rose high in front of them, with long sharp grasses and, every little while low round bushes clinging to the rocks. Higher up, the gray rock cliff rose as straight and unclimbable as glass.

They looked around the meadow. There was no sign, no "feel" of the path.

"Now where?" Raymond asked.

Bort's face was puzzled. "I'm not sure," he said. "I feel as if it should go straight across the meadow, but there's no sign."

"There's no way to climb that cliff," Raymond said, "so it must go back into the forest."

Merrily sat down in the middle of the meadow. "Why don't we stop and eat a little now. Maybe it will be easier to find the path after we've rested."

Raymond took Merrily's cloth bag from his shoulder. "You're right. I feel hungry, and I didn't even realize it. I wish I'd brought more food."

"Do you notice how the forest seems to be different on the other side of the meadow?" Bort said after a few bites of the sweetcake he'd taken from his bag.

Merrily and Raymond looked at the trees that grew up to the edge of the cliff and then back at the forest they'd just come through.

64

"It's thicker," Raymond said.

Merrily nodded. "The trees are thinner, and there's so much brush and so many bushes growing that it looks like a wall."

Bort slowly chewed his sweetcake and looked back and forth, first at the forest they'd just come through and then at the forest ahead of them. "It seems like the forest in front of us must be newer."

"Maybe it was burned a long time ago," Merrily said.

"Or planted," Bort said in puzzlement.

"The Finders?" Raymond asked tentatively, still afraid to believe they were for true.

"I wonder why . . ."

After they'd eaten, they stretched on their backs in the warm grass.

"What will we do when we find the Gartergates?" Bort asked.

"We'll know the old stories are for true," Raymond said dreamily. "But the very first thing . . . when we find the Gartergates, I want to climb to the top and see what's on the other side. If the Gartergates are for true, I want to know if the Weeuns are for true."

"The Weeuns—" Merrily began and stopped.

The Weeuns were nighttime terrors. In her memory, they hid under beds, threatened small Bulking children who didn't obey. Horrid little things. But if they really were for true . . . She shuddered and put the remains of their sweet-cakes into her cloth bag.

Bort began searching the edges of the meadow. He peered at the ground from close up, then from far away. First standing this way and then that way, looking at the trees, the cliff, even into the sky.

Merrily and Raymond walked behind him, searching

for some sign, anything out of the ordinary, something not natural.

"Bort, did you leave these stones like this?" Raymond asked, but he already knew that Bort hadn't. The rocks, three piled on top of each other in the same way that Bort had been stacking them to mark their way through the forest, were older, much older. They were moss-covered, like the rocks they'd found beside the remains of the path.

Bort ran back to where Raymond was standing.

"It's a marker," he said excitedly and slapped Raymond's back. "I think you've found the clue, Raymond!"

Merrily smiled at Raymond and shook her head.

"I must have walked past it ten times and never noticed it," she said.

"One of us would have found it sooner or later," Raymond said, trying not to show his pleasure.

Bort squatted on the ground and studied the pile of stones. They were only an arm's length from the sudden steep cliff that led up the Green Mountains. Bort peered along the edge of the cliff into the newer, denser forest.

"There's a very narrow space between the cliff and the forest," he said. "It's so well hidden it's like a secret tunnel."

The branches of the trees grew against the cliff and formed a roof. The tunnel was no wider than their bodies, maybe even narrower. Its length, what little they could see, was dark and shadowy.

"I'm sure this is the way," Bort said and entered the tunnel, hunching a little and pushing branches out of the way as he went.

Raymond started down the shadowy tunnel behind Bort. The trees of the forest grew close to the steep slope, but none grew in the strange, tunnel-like depression. He held the branches back until Merrily could grasp each one with her own hands. Bort leaned low and avoided most of the branches. He was soon several lengths ahead of Raymond and Merrily.

"Slow down," Raymond called ahead. His voice was startlingly loud in the silent tunnel.

"Shhh," Merrily said behind him.

The tunnel was eerily lighted. Little sun reached into it, and what did was colored a dull green by the trees and growth on one side and the gray rock on the other. As he cautiously stepped through the tunnel, Raymond's shoulder touched the rock cliff that rose as steeply as a wall. On the other side, the forest grew thick and tangled and seemed to reach out toward him.

Bort stopped in the tunnel and kicked at the moss-covered ground.

"I was wondering why there were no trees or bushes growing against the cliff," he said, half to himself. "Look at this."

The three of them squeezed together to look at the spot Bort had kicked bare of moss. Raymond's back was against the forest, and he felt the sharp scratchings of the branches through the cloth of his tunic.

"It's rock," Merrily exclaimed, bending down and touching the smooth gray stone that Bort had uncovered with his foot. Raymond knelt down a little further on and pulled back a patch of thick moss. There was more gray rock under the moss, but this time mortar lines were clearly visible between two slabs of rock: straight and smooth joints that allowed no trees or plants to take root.

"The Finders must have built it," Raymond said.

Bort nodded and pointed to the close impenetrable forest beside them.

"They must have laid the rocks to assure that there

would always be a way to the Gartergates without having to cut a new path."

"And then they planted the forest to hide the path," Raymond added.

Merrily was still bent over the spot that Bort had uncovered, but she was looking straight down the tunnel, frowning, her body frozen.

"What's wrong?" Raymond asked.

"I thought I saw something in the tunnel ahead of us." She shook her head, her voice just above a whisper. "It's hard to tell in this light, but I'm sure something ran across the path."

Raymond and Bort looked at each other over Merrily's head. Raymond thought he saw a flash of fear cross Bort's face.

Raymond looked down the path, squinting. "I don't see anything," he said, his own voice low.

"It's gone now," Merrily replied, and there was a catch, like a gasp, in her voice as she finished speaking.

Raymond stood and tried to nonchalantly brush bits of moss from his pants.

"It was just an animal, a rabbit or a mouseling. Animals always use old paths for their own wynds."

He laughed, sounding harsh and out of place in the close tunnel. "Animals are lazy. In a forest like this, so dense, they're not about to make new paths through the heavy bushes and tangles." He started off ahead of Bort and Merrily. "Let's find out what's beyond this."

Raymond hurried, pushing branches out of his way and letting them slap behind him.

"Ouch!" he heard Merrily exclaim, and then Bort saying, "Bend lower, and they won't hit you."

The tunnel felt too close, unsafe. There were no comforting tweak-bird sounds, no warm bits of sunlight. And there was no way out except backward or forward. The silent forest beside them was too thick to get through without hacking away the bushes and brush.

No wonder the animals used the tunnel; Raymond was sure that that was what Merrily had seen, a rabbit. He wished he'd had his slinger ready.

Abruptly the tunnel ended, and they were once again blinking their eyes in the bright sunshine of another meadow.

This meadow was larger than the meadow at the beginning of the tunnel but curiously shaped, like a funnel. The wide part was where Raymond and Merrily and Bort were standing. From there it narrowed into two knife edge cliffs that met in an unmistakable joining.

"It's them!"

"They're for true!"

"The Gartergates."

Merrily hugged herself, her face in a wide smile. Bort stood staring, his mouth moving without words. Suddenly Merrily took Bort's hands in her own and began to twirl him around the meadow in a crazy, uncontrolled dance.

"The Gartergates, the Gartergates. We've found the Gartergates," they chanted as they twirled.

Raymond laughed aloud as he watched Merrily pulling and tugging the slight Bort. Once she pulled him completely off the ground as they spun in quick, tight circles.

The Gartergates were for true. There was no mistaking the precise, square stones set up between the two cliffs. Raymond reached into his cloth bag and pulled out the Tiny that Gos had made and Wicker Bugle had given him. He held it in front of him and compared the two: the actual and the likeness.

Wicker Bugle must have made a drawing for Gos to copy because the likenesses were too exact. There were the same stones, larger square ones near the bottom, smaller ones near the top. The Gartergates were higher than he'd expected. He remembered the old stories: "full three times Glom Gloom high." Glom Gloom must have been a tall Bulking, as the old stories said. The only thing missing was the flock of geese flying under a cloud.

There were even vines growing along the rock cliffs on either side of the Gartergates. Obviously Wicker Bugle had been to the Gartergates. How else could she have told Gos how to make the Tiny? But now that he was seeing the Gartergates himself, Raymond felt a jealousy that anyone else should have found them first. He felt pride, as if he had had some part in their construction. Hadn't he rediscovered them?

Merrily and Bort danced back to him and collapsed, laughing, on the ground.

"Who shall we tell first?" Merrily asked. "We'll be heroes, and the stolen map will be unimportant once it's understood why it was taken."

Raymond turned to her so angrily that her laughter and smiles stopped like death.

"No one," he shouted, raising his fist. "If you even say the word, 'Gartergates,' in front of anyone . . ."

"Raymond," Bort said quietly, his face white.

Raymond paused and looked at their two frightened faces.

He turned away. "I'm sorry."

"It's all right," Merrily said.

"We can't tell anyone else yet. Who would believe us any more than they believe Wicker Bugle? We have to discover why the Gartergates were built."

Merrily breathed in sharply, and Raymond turned back to her.

"You really do plan on discovering if the Weeuns are for true, don't you?" she asked, looking up at the silvery stones of the Gartergates.

Raymond nodded. "Why else should we tell anyone about the Gartergates? If the Weeuns aren't for true, there's no reason to keep the Gartergates strong, is there?"

"I suppose not," Merrily said doubtfully, "but still . . ."

Raymond bit his lip and tried to think of something else. One careless word to the Majester's daughter, Trillia, or worse yet, to her parents, could ruin everything.

"We won't mention a word of the Gartergates to anyone," Bort said firmly.

Merrily turned first to Bort, then to Raymond, then shook her head.

"Not to anyone," she agreed.

10 · The Climb

RAYMOND set his cloth bag under a low tree at the edge of the meadow and turned to Merrily.

"I'm going to climb the Gartergates. You stay here with our bags."

Merrily's face reddened.

"I'm not a baby watcher. If you're going to climb the Gartergates, I'm coming with you. There's no reason to stay with the bags."

Raymond looked at Bort. Bort shrugged and looked down at his hands.

"I intend to climb the Gartergates with you also."

Merrily was as stubborn as Raymond, and Bort was as stubborn as Merrily.

"All right," Raymond said. "We'll leave our bags here and try to find a way up the Gartergates."

The Gartergates rose sheer and smooth. There wasn't even room for a toehold in the mortared cracks. On the west side, where the edge joined to the cliff, it was as smooth as the corner of a house. But the other side seemed to have a slight slope to it, and the rocks weren't as evenly joined.

Raymond spit on his hands.

"I think we might be able to go up this way."

Bort shaded his eyes and peered above them. "There

do seem to be spaces between the rocks further up, almost like toe- and handholds."

It was hard to find spaces to fit feet and hands. Merrily waited until Raymond was the length of his body up the cliff before she began following him, then Bort followed her, keeping himself a little to the side of both Merrily and Raymond, so that it wasn't long before Bort was even with Merrily, then passing her slowly, carefully inching his way, seeming to slip less then either Raymond or Merrily.

Raymond hugged the rocks of the Gartergates, feeling the warm stones against his chest. He balanced himself, both feet in tiny gaps between the rocks and one hand gripping tightly to another crack while his other hand felt blindly above him for another hold.

Before long they had broken fingernails and their hands were scraped raw from fitting them between the rocks.

Two-thirds of the way to the top, Raymond gripped a protruding stone with his hands and pulled himself up, using his entire body's weight as he tried to find a toehold. The stone suddenly moved. It teetered and pulled loose from the cliff, crashing past him. For part of an instant he scrambled, trying to stay on the cliff, frantically feeling for a toehold, another handhold. There was nothing.

"Look out!" he shouted to Merrily beneath him, but it was too late.

He fell helplessly down the cliff, rolling against the rock, feeling it bruise his chest and arms, his legs. There was a squeal of pain and surprise as he hit Merrily, and they rolled the rest of the way to the ground, flailing against each other and the rocks.

They sprawled at the bottom of the Gartergates, stunned, trying to catch their breath. Merrily's foot was against Raymond's head, and he could tell that there would soon be a swelling above his left eye. There was blood along one of Merrily's arms, trickling to her wrist and onto the grass.

"Are you safe?" Bort shouted down to them. "Shall I come down?"

Raymond couldn't catch his breath to answer, but he waved his arm to Bort where he hung against the rock like a winger walking up a wall.

"I'm . . . all . . . right," Merrily said uncertainly. She touched the blood on her arm. "It's only a scrape . . . I think."

Raymond sat up and moved his arms and legs; every joint moved and worked the way it should. There was a tender spot on his cheek, and his eye throbbed.

He leaned over Merrily. Her face was as pale as the inside of a river shell. But she wasn't crying; he didn't know what he'd do if she were crying.

"Let me see," he said, motioning to her arm. Her hand was gripping her forearm. Red blood showed between her fingers.

She took her hand from her arm and wiped the blood off on the grass. There was a deep gash beneath her elbow, spilling with blood.

"That needs bandaging," Raymond said.

"With what?" Merrily asked.

"Here," Raymond said and pulled off his already ripped tunic.

"You can't do that. What will your mother say?"

"Not as much as yours would if we ripped your tunic," Raymond told her.

He ripped the heavy cloth of his tunic along the edge

of the torn sleeve. With his teeth he tore it into a bandage-sized strip.

"Raymond!" Bort called from above them. "It's a hollow!"

Raymond stood, the torn tunic in one hand and the strip of cloth in the other.

"Where?"

He could see Bort, the upper half of his body inside the hole made by the stone that had pulled loose when Raymond fell. Merrily jumped up and stood beside him, her hand holding her bleeding arm.

"He says it's a hollow," Raymond told her. He quickly wrapped the piece of cloth around her arm, encircling the gash twice and tying it firmly. Bort's legs waved in the air as he fit his body into the opening. They could hear his muffled voice calling back to them, but they couldn't make out the words.

"I want to go up there," Merrily said excitedly.

Raymond put his hand on her arm. "Don't be foolish. Let's wait to hear what Bort finds."

Bort pulled himself into the hollow until only his feet showed, sticking out from the smooth gray rock as if they were imbedded there. He was talking, but as hard as they strained, they couldn't make out what he was saying.

"I wish he'd just hush up until he got down here," Merrily said.

"Quiet, now," Raymond said, although he couldn't hear Bort either.

Bort reappeared. First his legs and then the bottom half of his body as his feet searched and found toeholds. Finally his upper body and head.

"What's he carrying?" Merrily asked.

"I don't know. It looks like a stick."

Out of the hollow, Bort stood against the Gartergates and arranged something upon his chest. In one hand he held a long stick, longer than his body.

Then he swiftly turned onto his back and slid down the cliff to them, the stick held high and the other thing clutched against his chest. Stones clattered about him as he landed. His face was streaked with dust and sweat.

"What is it? What is it?" Merrily cried.

"I'm not sure yet, but it's old, very old."

Bort held out the stick to Raymond.

It was so thick Raymond's fingers didn't quite meet when he put his hand around it, and it was as tall as Raymond and worn smooth. When Raymond rubbed it with his hands, the dust fell away, and the wood shone warmly. The whorls and grain of the wood seemed almost polished. The top of the stick was bent and thicker, even smoother than the lower part of the stick. The other end was carved into a round knob.

"It looks like a crutch, doesn't it?" Raymond said. "What else did you find?"

Bort held up a bag, rather like their cloth bags, but made from a heavy material. It was gray and stiff and cracked along the drawstring top. Whatever was inside made it bulge at the bottom.

"Should we open it?" Bort asked.

Bort held the bag out in front of him. It was slightly bigger than Raymond's bag, and the strange material made it mysterious and foreign. Surely it had been hidden for a reason. Perhaps what was inside wasn't meant to be seen by any Bulking.

Raymond thought of the Majester in his braggy new

house, of the Bulkings who didn't believe in the Gartergates or Glom Gloom any longer, of his own mother who didn't think there was an outside.

"Let's open it," he said. "We've found it, and that gives us the right."

They sat on the grass facing each other, and Bort placed the bag in the middle. Raymond gently opened the drawstring top. Bits of the bag and dust fell away as the gap between the strings widened.

The open bag looked pitiful and dirty. Too ordinary.

"The Finders . . ." Merrily said and then was silent.

Raymond reached inside the bag. Bort leaned forward, and Merrily leaned back, away.

He pulled out another bag, only this one was small and made of cloth, shaped like a cylinder by whatever was inside. Raymond loosened the little bag's drawstring and took out the object.

"A spyglass," said Bort. A spyglass had been one of his greatest desires since he was a little grader.

It was a dull black spyglass, worn to a polished silver where other hands had held it. The glass at either end still sparkled in the sun. Whoever had put it away for the last time had given it a deep farewell polish.

Raymond held it against his eye.

"Powerful," he said and pulled it away, squinting.

He could see that Bort was eager to touch it, to try it. He started to hand it over when the sunlight caught and picked out faint lines along the side. He pulled it back from Bort's outstretched hand.

"There's writing on the side of it," he said.

He rubbed his sleeve across the writing, trying to make it stand out. The letters were formed in an old style of writing with curls and twists.

Bort and Merrily leaned forward, watching him impatiently.

"Bort!" he said. "The writing on the spy glass reads, B. D. Gard!"

11 · Wicker Bugle

O. GARD," Bort repeated, his eyes wide. "How could that be?"

"Could it be one of your great-greats, Bort?" Merrily asked.

"I don't know. I've never heard mention of any of my great-greats," Bort said.

"But have any of us?" Raymond asked. "Our parents never talk about their parents or the parents before them. They're forgotten as soon as they're dead."

He looked at Bort with new interest. What kind of Bulkings were in Bort's past?

"It *has* to be one of your great-greats, Bort," he said with finality.

Raymond placed the spyglass in Bort's open hands. Merrily watched solemnly as Bort took the spyglass and held it reverently, his eyes shining.

There was only one other object in the bag, and Raymond placed it on the grass in front of them.

"It's a book," Merrily said, touching the stained cover, which was made of the same kind of material as the bag. The corners of the book were flaking away into a fine dust, like the edges of the bag.

"There's nothing else," Raymond said. He nodded to Merrily. "Go ahead and open it."

Raymond had hoped for something more dramatic: a

mysterious treasure or some positive proof of the Finders or the Weeuns. Not a spyglass, a book and an old crutch.

The book crackled as Merrily gently opened it. The pages were made of a heavy, heavy paper and were filled with lines of tiny writing. Writing that began at the very corner of the page and continued from edge to edge, never skipping a line or space so that the top of a letter touched the bottom of the line above it and the bottom of that letter touched the top of the line below it. The writing was neat and fine, each letter perfectly formed. But the words made no sense.

"It's written in some other language," Merrily said in disappointment.

Bort looked closely at a page of writing. "But I recognize all the letters. Could the Finders have spoken a different language?"

"Maybe the Finders didn't write this," Raymond suggested.

Merrily continued to gently turn page after page, "Look at this!"

It was a drawing of the map that Raymond had taken from Gimly School, without all the lovely coloring and details, but an identical map just the same. Instead of a tiny flock of geese winging over the location of the Gartergates, there was a drawing of the Gartergates themselves and the funnel-shaped meadow.

"It has to have been written by one of the Finders," Merrily said as they gazed at the map's tiny inked stones laid up one on top of the other.

"Do you think that this writing," Raymond asked tentatively, "could possibly be using all the letters we know but arranged so that no one but those who understood could read it?"

Bort and Merrily looked excitedly at Raymond.

"That's it! A secret language!"

"But why?"

"Let's see if the whole book is in the secret language," Raymond said.

Merrily continued to turn the pages, softly, one after the other so they wouldn't crack. Page after page filled with the tiny, close writing. There was a picture of a tweak-bird on another page, then a picture that Raymond thought looked like a young Tailor Tree. There were even pictures of vegetables: paturnies, matoes, carrots. All surrounded by the cramped, mysterious writing.

Finally they came to the last written page, a page of shakier, less neat writing. At the bottom of the page was a signature.

"Rival . . . no . . . Royal . . . Royal Bugle," Merrily read aloud.

They looked at each other. Another name that sounded too familiar.

"Royal Bugle? Wicker Bugle . . . do you think?" Bort asked.

"She knew about the Gartergates," Raymond answered. "She knew they were for true before we did. Maybe her great-greats told her about their past; maybe she's known about the true Gartergates for a long, long time."

"Perhaps Wicker Bugle isn't such a crazy old haggie after all," Merrily said.

"I most certainly am not."

Merrily slammed the book shut and put it behind her back. Bort slipped the spyglass inside his tunic, and Raymond quickly shoved the bag beneath his legs.

"It's too late for that. I've been watching you since you

began climbing the Gartergates," Wicker Bugle said as she emerged from the edge of the forest.

They didn't move or speak. Wicker Bugle stood over them, slightly hunched; her long, thin body covered with the same gray clothes Raymond remembered seeing on her since he was a child. She laughed softly, looking at each of them in turn, her eyes finally resting on Raymond.

"You, Raymond Fibbey," she said, pointing a bony finger at him," you are a Bulking of action. You do your great-greats proud.'"

A "Bulking of action," sounded like a title, an honor, the way Wicker Bugle said it.

"What do you mean, my great-greats?" Raymond asked her. "What do you know about them?"

"I know about the great-greats of all three of you. And of many more besides." She shook her fist. "The Bulkings of Waterpushin have pushed aside their memories, their old stories. They only remember for the sake of their holidays, and even then they can't recall why they're celebrating. But I haven't forgotten, and I won't let them forget either."

Her eyes burned fiercely. "Now you three must make them remember also. There is much danger ahead if the Bulkings don't awaken and look to their safety."

Wicker Bugle had been saying the same thing on the corners of the cobbies and in the square forever. Yet nothing had ever happened.

"What kind of danger?" Merrily asked patiently.

Wicker Bugle raised her arm and pointed to the Gartergates rising above them in the late morning sun.

She repeated the warning of the old legend:

> *And now remember the Gartergates,*
> *Full three times Glom Gloom high,*

When strong they be, no harm to ye,
But left to lie, prepare to die.

She said the last line so menacingly, so coldly, that Raymond felt chilled. He forced himself to say calmly, "But the Gartergates *are* strong. We could find no weaknesses. And if you've been watching us as long as you say you have, you saw how difficult it was to climb the little way we did."

With her lightning changes of mood, Wicker Bugle looked gently at Raymond and said, "Aye, but do you know what's happening on the other side of the Gartergates?"

Raymond shook his head. "Do you?"

Wicker Bugle also shook her head, but sadly.

"I've tried to climb the Gartergates many times," she said. "Not as often now as when I was younger, but I have never been able to climb past the place where you pulled the rock free. The Gartergates are unclimbable past that spot." She looked up at the hollow. "Now I know why."

She shook her head again. "No . . . No, I don't know what's on the other side, but I *feel* something."

She sat down between Raymond and Merrily, crossing her legs like a young Bulking child. Merrily edged away from her, and Wicker Bugle turned to Merrily, smiling so reassuringly that Merrily stopped, sheepishly returning the smile.

"Sometimes," Wicker Bugle said to them, "I feel things before they happen. The early passage of Warm Days. The sudden flight of the geese before the seasons change. A fish netter who won't return. A sorrow between families." She closed her eyes and swayed slightly.

"And now I see that a great danger could come upon Waterpushin like a moonless night dropping on a sunlit day. There are strange scrabblings and terrible hungers. A great hunger that gnaws—"

"Oh, stop!" Merrily cried, covering her ears with her hands.

Wicker Bugle sat up straight, blinking her eyes as if she had been asleep. She put her hand on Merrily's shoulder. Merrily pulled away from the hand, and Wicker Bugle did not try to touch her again but said kindly, "I'm sorry, Merrily. I be forgetting how I sound. Will you forgive me?"

Merrily lifted her head and looked into Wicker Bugle's eyes. She saw only the gentle old eyes of a sorrowful woman. The frightening face was gone. Merrily nodded.

"Thank you," Wicker Bugle said and turned to Raymond and Bort. "Do I be frightening you two, now?"

"Not I," said Raymond, swallowing past the hard lump he felt in his throat.

"Nor I," added Bort in a whisper.

"Good," said Wicker Bugle. "Now let's be on with it."

She placed her hands on her knees and said briskly, "I know how to read the secret language. I have Royal Bugle's other books at my home. You thought right when you guessed he was my great-great.

"I always knew there was one more book," Wicker Bugle continued, "but I could never find it. I searched and searched and read and reread the other books, looking for a clue as to where it was, but found nothing."

"And we have found it," Bort said softly.

"Aye. It is the last book: the story of the Finders and the Finding of Waterpushin. The other books end just before the Finding and the escape from the Weeuns, with only the reassurance that the truth of the escape must be kept precious to the Bulkings."

"Then why write it in a secret language and hide it in

the Gartergates where no Bulking could find it?" Raymond asked.

"Royal Bugle was a private man who began as a private child," Wicker Bugle said patiently. "He says in his other books that he had a bothersome brother and sister who were always into his things so he had need to keep his thoughts private."

"And they couldn't read his secret language," Merrily said.

A brother *and* a sister. In all the Bulking families Raymond knew, there was only one child or two, almost never three.

"Aye," said Wicker Bugle. "It is a habit he kept as a Bulking man. Royal Bugle said the story as he wrote it in Bulking language would be kept by the Bulking leaders, and he would hide his copy in the secret language, should danger fall and the Bulkings have need of the secret copy. Clues would be left, he said—"

"But they were lost, the same as the meaning of the geese on the maps," Bort said.

"Lost . . ." she repeated, looking up at the Gartergates where the rock had pulled loose and left the hollow.

"But where is the copy Royal Bugle made for the Bulking leaders, the one in Bulking language?" Raymond asked.

"Lost also," Wicker Bugle said. "I have never heard tell of it, have you?"

Merrily, Bort and Raymond shook their heads. They had never heard even the slightest mention of a book, only old, old stories of a long-ago adventure that gave them a holiday.

"You took the map, Raymond Fibbcy?"

"I did."

Wicker Bugle nodded. "It was needed."

"I would like to read the last book," she told them.

Merrily took the book from behind her, but held it tightly against herself, wrapping her arms around it.

"How do we know you won't just keep it?" she asked.

"Wouldn't I have the right, if I wanted?"

Merrily looked at her glumly. Finders keepers, she thought.

"You can't read it yourselves," Wicker Bugle said. "Only I can read it."

Bort took the spyglass from his tunic and held it out.

"The name engraved on the spyglass is B. D. Gard. Do you know who that was?"

"Aye. Your great-great was a trusted and true friend of Glom Gloom. It was his spyglass. It is right that it be yours now. You may have need . . ."

Suddenly Wicker Bugle stood up in a flap of gray clothes and an untangling of long limbs.

"Come with me to my house," she said, her arms waving. "I will show you the other books of Royal Bugle, and once you have seen them, you can decide whether I'm a trustworthy crazy old haggie."

Merrily blushed red, and Wicker Bugle chuckled.

"Don't be feeling bad now. Don't you think I know that's what they call me: a crazy old haggie?"

"Now?" Raymond asked, thinking of another try at climbing the Gartergates.

"I think it best you know the truth as soon as possible. And asides," she pointed first at Merrily, then at Raymond, "don't you think it would be a good idea if we looked to those wounds of yours?"

Raymond touched the swelling above his eye, and Merrily looked down at the stained strip of Raymond's tunic wrapped around her forearm. In the excitement of their discovery, they had forgotten their fall from the Garter-gates.

"I agree with her, Raymond," Bort added.

Wicker Bugle smiled and clapped her hands together.

"Good, good. We'll lunch in my garden." She made shooing motions with her hands. "Hurry now, so we'll have time to talk."

There were only two cloth bags under the tree. Bort's was gone.

"It has to be here," Raymond said as Bort stood staring at the ground. "Are you sure you left it under the tree?"

"I'm positive. I dropped it right here beside Merrily's bag."

"Do you think *she* might have taken it?" Merrily whispered to Raymond.

Wicker Bugle walked over to where they stood.

"What's taking you such a while?" she asked.

"Bort's bag is gone," Raymond told her. "Did you move it?"

"Where was it?" Wicker Bugle asked, her voice sharp.

Bort pointed to the ground under the tree. "Right there, beside Merrily's bag."

Wicker Bugle got down on her hands and knees and peered among the grass, her face close to the ground.

Bort looked at Raymond and raised his eyebrows. Raymond shrugged. Who knew what to expect from Wicker Bugle?

"Ahhh," Wicker Bugle breathed. "Here's where it was dragged away."

Sure enough, when they looked closely, they could see where the grass was parted, and a length away was a smudge on the bare earth where something had been dragged across it.

"What did it?" Bort asked. "The marks from the bag cover any tracks."

Merrily pointed into the thick trees.

"It looks as if it was pulled into the woods. We'll never find it in there."

"Some animal must have dragged it away for the food," Raymond suggested.

"I'm sorry to lose my net-mending knife, but the rest doesn't matter," Bort said.

Wicker Bugle's brows were pulled together in a deep frown, but she said nothing. She stood so long, looking first at them, then at the ground and the forest that Raymond finally asked, "Well, are we going to your house or not?"

"Aye. Let's leave now," Wicker Bugle said slowly.

Bort put the spyglass back inside its little cloth bag and slipped it inside his tunic. Merrily carefully replaced the book in the old bag and carried it against her body, instead of by its strings. Raymond put both his and Merrily's bags over his shoulder.

Wicker Bugle led the way toward the tunnel. At its shadowy entrance she turned and surveyed the three of them.

"Don't be forgetting the stick that Bort took from the hollow," she said to Raymond.

Raymond looked at her in surprise. "But that's just an old crutch."

Wicker Bugle threw back her head and laughed loudly while they looked on uncomfortably.

"Just an old crutch . . ." she repeated, laughing again and shaking her head. ". . . just an old crutch . . . That, my dear Bulking child, is Glom Gloom's crooky-staff."

12 · With Wicker Bugle

THEY HURRIED through the woods single file. Wicker Bugle in front, then Bort, Merrily and, lastly, Raymond. It seemed to Raymond that they were following Wicker Bugle haphazardly through the forest. He couldn't "feel" any type of trail as he had when he and Bort and Merrily had found the Garter-gates.

He hoped Wicker Bugle wouldn't go into one of her "moods" and leave them stranded in the forest. Bort, he saw, was looking carefully to either side. Surely he wouldn't forget the way.

Raymond carried the crooky-staff, if that's what it really was, like a walking stick. His hand naturally held it at a level where there seemed to be an extra polished knobby area. Where a tall Bulking's hand might just grip the crooky-staff if it were used like a crutch, with the bent end under a shoulder.

Is that how Glom Gloom used the crooky-staff, like a crutch? In the old stories he'd used it like a proud staff, to lean on when he was weary, to thrust bushes and vines out of his way as he strode the Green Mountains in search of Waterpushin. In the old stories, Glom Gloom was always pictured with his crooky-staff by his side, a straight, noble crooky-staff, carved with intricate whorls and made of the finest wood. Not with a bent top to fit under a shoulder.

Not a plain and stout stick that could have been made from any tree in the forests.

Wicker Bugle stopped. She peered into the woods about her and seemed to be listening. Bort and Merrily and Raymond stopped a little behind, wondering what she might do next.

From around the side of a mound stepped a golden deer. It stopped a few lengths from Wicker Bugle, its nose quivering and its feet stepping nervously back and forth, back and forth. It blew through its nose, and Wicker Bugle laughed.

"You won't scare them off that easy, my friend." She held out a sweet she'd taken from a pocket hidden somewhere in her loose gray clothes.

"Tck, tck, tck," she clucked to the deer.

The deer daintily came forward, pausing every few steps to blow through its nose.

Raymond, Merrily and Bort held their breath and didn't dare move. They had never seen a deer so close, only glimpses of the delicate creatures as they ran in the opposite direction, bounding in great, graceful leaps, their tails up and showing white, taunting undersides.

When the deer was close enough, it stretched its neck and took the sweet from Wicker Bugle's palm, its soft lips barely touching her skin. Then it turned in a flash and bounded off into the forest. They watched as its tail flipped up white and disappeared.

They looked at Wicker Bugle in wonder. Had any Bulking ever been so close to a deer? A deer for a friend? It was a wonderful mystery.

"It was beautiful," Merrily said. "Is it a pet of yours?"

"As much as any wild thing can be a pet," Wicker Bugle

said, stepping onto a path that went toward the mound from which the deer had come.

The mound was taller than Raymond and as big around as his mother's garden. It was covered all over with bright flowers and vines, smelling sweetly in the sun. Who had made such a large pile of dirt in the middle of the forest?

The path stopped in front of the mound. Wicker Bugle reached through the vines and flowers and pushed open a door. They gasped, and Wicker Bugle chortled in delight, watching their amazed faces.

"What is it?" Bort asked.

"Have you never been inside a house in the ground?" Wicker Bugle asked as she stepped inside, motioning for them to follow.

Wicker Bugle's house was one large room shaped like an upside-down bowl. Raymond had expected it to be dark inside; but once he was standing in the center of the room, he saw there were windows at different heights at several places around the sloping walls. Vines grew around and in front of some of the windows so the light that filtered through them was a soft yellow-green. The furnishings in the house all were soft and roundish in the warm light.

There was a bed on one side, with a row of dresses, all alike, hanging beside it. On the other side was a small cupboard and a fireplace. A table stood in front of the fireplace, with two chairs beside it.

And everywhere, on shelves, in piles on the floor, under the bed, were books. Large ones, small ones, some in disrepair and some that looked new. Some were open face-down and some had their places held by other books. There were more books than in the Waterpushin Library.

"Let's see to your wounds now," Wicker Bugle said. "Sit down here, both of you."

Merrily touched the seat of the chair before she sat down. It was made from the same strange material as the bag and the cover of Royal Bugle's last book. It felt smooth and cool under her fingers, and it gave slightly when she sat on it.

"You'd better take off that tunic and let me see if I can repair it," Wicker Bugle said to Raymond.

"It's beyond repair," Raymond told her.

"Let me try to clean it up then," she said.

"It's fine," Raymond said curtly.

Wicker Bugle shrugged. "As you wish. Come with me, Bort."

On the opposite side of the room Wicker Bugle opened another nearly invisible door. Bright sunshine entered the room, and she and Bort went outside.

Merrily and Raymond could hear their voices, mainly Wicker Bugle's, accompanied by the sounds of splashing water.

"I think she's nice," Merrily said, "in a strange sort of way."

"She's all right."

"All these books . . . Do you think she's read them all?"

"Maybe."

"I wonder what it's like to live in a house like this," Merrily tried again.

Raymond didn't answer, and Merrily began to unwind the bandage from her arm. She paused, looking at the dirty, bloody bandage, then at Raymond's torn tunic. She smiled at Raymond.

"Thank you for bandaging my arm."

Raymond nodded and looked away.

Wicker Bugle gently washed the dried blood from Merrily's arm, clucking to herself and saying, "There, there," when Merrily winced. When the gash was clean, she spread a thin layer of clear ointment on it and wrapped a clean bandage around Merrily's arm.

"In a day or two you won't even know it's there," she said to Merrily, patting her knee. "Now go outside and wash your face and straighten your clothes. Bort will show you how to draw the water."

"I don't need any bandaging, and I can wash myself," Raymond said to Wicker Bugle as she dipped her cloth in the basin.

Wicker Bugle continued to wring out the cloth and chuckled softly. "I wouldn't try to bandage a prickly young Bulking like you, Raymond Fibbey. I'd be more likely to prick myself on your sharp spines than to do you any good."

She took a blue bottle from her cupboard and poured a little liquid on the cloth. "Here, put this on that bump over your eye."

Raymond made no move to take it. Wicker Bugle sighed.

"It'll keep down the swelling—and the questions."

Raymond took the cloth and put it on the swelling above his eye. It *did* feel soothing.

"Is the map well hidden?" Wicker Bugle suddenly asked.

"Aye."

"Keep it so," she said.

Wicker Bugle took plates and cups from the cupboard and set them on a tray, then took a pitcher of cold berry water from a cupboard in the floor.

"Did *you* build this house?" Raymond asked.

93

"Oh, no," she answered. "Royal Bugle built it after the Finding was over and done with. He was a bit of a lone Bulking. In his books he says other Bulkings thought he was a little . . ." She smiled. ". . . crazy."

"Did all these books belong to him?"

Merrily came back inside, and Wicker Bugle motioned for her to take some apples and sweetcakes.

"Most of them probably belonged to him. He brought them to Waterpushin from the Widelands."

"The Widelands—" Raymond began, but Wicker Bugle raised her hand to silence him.

"I'll tell you all I know, but first let's be eating our lunch in the garden." She handed a heaping tray to Raymond. "I think we'll be able to make up for Bort's missing food."

In the garden, flowers and vines and sticky roses all grew together in a wild tumble of color. The flowers ringed a grassy area where a rough table and benches were placed under a tree with broad green leaves. Honey wingers were buzzing about the flowers in the warm sunshine.

Merrily sat with the bag containing Royal Bugle's last book close beside her. They ate in silence: hard egg sandwiches and cold paturnies, delicious chewy sweetcakes. Once Raymond started to ask again about the Widelands, but Wicker Bugle held up her hand.

"After lunch," she said firmly.

Finally, Wicker Bugle pushed her plate away and asked, "What would you like to know first?"

"Where are the Widelands?"

"Why did Royal Bugle hide these things in the Gartergates?"

"Is this Glom Gloom's crooky-staff, for true? How did he use it?"

"What happened to the Weeuns?"

94

Wicker Bugle held up her hands. "Stop. Stop. Perhaps it would be best if I tell you how I came to know as much as I do."

"I know where I've seen a tree like this before," Bort said suddenly. "The Tailor Tree."

Wicker Bugle nodded. "That's right. They're sisters, or brothers, if you like. Royal Bugle wrote that he planted them both as seedlings he'd brought from the Widelands."

"As a child I lived here alone with my father," Wicker Bugle began. "My mother died before I can remember. When I had seen twelve seasons, my father took me to the Gartergates. He showed me how the great stones had been carefully mortared together to keep out the Weeuns. But even he didn't know the details. His own father had shown him the Gartergates when he was twelve, and his father's father before him. But they too had been caught up in the forgetting of the other Bulkings. The Gartergates were strong. Why should any Bulking worry about an old story?

"When we returned home, my father took down two books from the highest shelf. 'Our great-great, Royal Bugle,' my father said, 'wrote the story of Waterpushin in these books in a secret language. None of his children's children have ever been able to read them. No matter, they are a treasure, and when I am gone, they will be yours to pass on.'"

Wicker Bugle looked up into the leaves of the Tailor Tree's sister.

"Only a season later my father died. I refused to go down into Waterpushin to live. This was the only place I'd ever known. That mayhap be when the Bulkings began to think of me as crazy. The few who did come up here took back tales that I was living in a hole in the ground, like a rabbit.

"But I stayed on here, and after a few seasons they stopped bothering me. I have my garden and my books, and what else I need Gos does for me in trade for herbs and vegetables.

"I was determined to find the Gartergates again and to learn Royal Bugle's secret language. Since I'd paid no attention to the way my father had taken me, finding the Gartergates seemed nigh impossible. But I didn't give up. I was a grown woman before I found them again, after seasons and seasons of searching and going over and over the same ground.

"Learning the secret languages took even longer. Royal Bugle was a clever Bulking, and he kept changing the meanings of each letter, so I'd have part of a book read and then discover he'd changed the meanings. I'd have to start learning a secret language all over again."

"What did Royal Bugle say?" Raymond asked.

"Ah, Raymond Fibbey," Wicker Bugle said. "You be just like your great-great. Rushing to the end before the beginning has begun."

Merrily frowned at Raymond and turned to Wicker Bugle. "Please go on. We want to hear the entire story."

"There were three who were the best of friends and comrades from the beginning to the end," Wicker Bugle continued. "Glom Gloom, Royal Bugle and Bartholomew Dare Gard—your great-great, Bort. They were the Finders."

Bort squirmed and beamed pridefully as he touched the bulk in his tunic that was the spy glass.

"The Bulkings lived peacefully in the Widelands until one day a great boat of Weeuns came from the Bluey Seas. The Bulkings had never seen any folk different from themselves, and at first they tried to welcome the littler folk, ready to make room in their villages and homes.

"But the Weeuns were a vicious and cruel people. They had a strange power over the Bulkings; Royal Bugle said it was a power of their eyes and voices to turn the Bulkings to the Weeuns' will, like a hypnotism. And asides, the Weeuns were a warring folk. Bulkings had never known any enemies. Bulkings do not kill. They tried hiding from the Weeuns, but that was like trying to hide the Tailor Tree in the Mid-cobbie.

"The Weeuns, with their powerful voices and eyes, enslaved the Bulkings. The Bulkings lived at their mercy."

Wicker Bugle's voice softened to a whisper, and she stared away at nothing, her face still.

"And Glom Gloom saved them?" Raymond prompted.

Wicker Bugle looked at Raymond in surprise, and then her eyes went quiet again.

"Sometimes, during a troubled age, one who would not otherwise be a leader is forced into becoming a leader . . . a great leader."

"What did he do?" Merrily asked eagerly, but Wicker Bugle went on as if she hadn't heard.

"Glom Gloom was a solitary Bulking, a leather-maker."

"What is leather?"

Wicker Bugle pointed to the bag beside Merrily that contained the book of Royal Bugle.

"That bag is made of leather. It's from the skin of a deer."

Merrily shuddered, thinking of the little deer they'd seen outside Wicker Bugle's strange home.

"My great-great, Royal Bugle, was a hunter of wild animals. In those days a few Bulkings still ate meat, although the hunters and killers of wild animals were outcasts. Bulkings who ate meat wanted to have it delivered to their homes already cut up and disguised. The actual hunting and killing was something no one wanted to think about.

"Glom Gloom used the hides from the animals Royal Bugle killed to make bags and even shoes and the backs of books.

"Bartholomew Dare Gard, whose eyes were as sharp as a night bird's, hunted with Royal Bugle, although he himself didn't kill any animals. He could spot a deer from further off than any other Bulking."

"Did they live together?" Bort asked.

Wicker Bugle shook her head. "All three were solitary Bulkings. They each lived alone, apart from other Bulkings, but not far from each other. They had that special, respectful friendship that solitary people have. My great-great mentions several times in his books of the Bulking children coming to visit, of the village men coming to bring grog. It was their trade that set them apart, not their manner."

"Why didn't they do something else, then?"

"A trade was handed down from father to son, much as it is now. Glom Gloom's father had been a leather-worker. Royal Bugle's father had been a hunter. Royal Bugle's books do not say what Bartholomew Dare Gard's trade was, only that he was a good and true friend of smallish stature and keen eye.

"Because they were solitary, they did not come under the attack or to the attention of the Weeuns as the other Bulkings did. They were good Bulking men who cared for the Bulkings and the Bulking way of life, no matter that they might be outcasts. The three planned and thought and thought of a way to save their fellow Bulkings who were enslaved by the Weeuns. The only solution was to find a place to move everyone where the Weeuns couldn't find them. Somewhere where the Bulkings would be safe to live their peaceful lives by their own customs.

"They searched and searched. Royal Bugle says that Glom Gloom searched from darkness to darkness, refusing to give up and making his limp worse by his constant walking and climbing."

"The crooky-staff *was* a crutch, then!" Raymond said.

"Aye. Then one day, Glom Gloom was caught in the Green Mountains in a pouring-down rainstorm. He was on the edge of a steep cliff when his crutch slipped in the mud and he fell down the sheer, rain-soaked rocks. When he recovered himself, he discovered he was in the little meadow where the tunnel opens into the Gartergates."

Merrily clapped her hands. "And he was the Finder of Waterpushin!"

"Aye. He spent day after day exploring the edges of Waterpushin until he was satisfied there was no way out except the break in the cliff where he had fallen. Then he returned to Royal Bugle and Bartholomew Dare Gard, who thought he'd been killed or lost forever. Royal Bugle describes their celebration at his return in his book. How they talked and talked of the land Glom Gloom had found, planning and congratulating each other.

"The three Finders moved immediately to Waterpushin and began laying out plans for the village, the crops, and most importantly, for the Gartergates."

Wicker Bugle paused and thoughtfully rubbed her cheek.

"How did the Bulkings escape from the Weeuns?" Raymond asked. "From the powerful eyes and voices?"

Wicker Bugle sighed. "That I don't know. The book ends there. The only other clue is a piece of paper Royal

Bugle wrote and slipped between the pages, saying he was the last left alive and he had hidden certain artifacts for future Bulkings, should the book in Bulking language be lost and the Bulkings have need of the old secrets. He then listed names of Bulkings whose bravery should never be forgotten."

Wicker Bugle paused and looked at Merrily.

"In that list is, 'Sullivan Cumbers.' "

Then she looked at Raymond and smiled faintly.

"At the very end of the list, Royal Bugle wrote, 'and to the impatient, distruthful Wilder Fibbey, to whom we perhaps all owe our lives.' "

13 · The Majester's New House

*T*HE *distruthful* Wilder Fibbey?" Raymond repeated.

Merrily covered her mouth, and Bort
turned his head so Raymond couldn't see his face.

"I'm afraid so," said Wicker Bugle. "It seems as if some
of the characteristics of our great-greats have come down
to each of us. My solitary Royal Bugle. Bort's keen-eyed
Bartholomew Dare Gard. Raymond's impatient," she kindly
left off the word "distruthful," Wilder Fibbey. I don't know
about your great-great; Merrily, other than his name; but I
would guess from knowing you, that he was an undaunted
adventurer."

They sat silently in the shade of the Tailor Tree's sister, thinking of the Finders, the old stories that were becoming for true, if slightly altered from the grand mystical
stories they had learned.

"Will you be letting me have my great-great's book,
now?" Wicker Bugle abruptly asked.

They each waited for the other to speak. Merrily held
the leather bag close to her body, wrapping her arms
around it.

Wicker Bugle reached toward Merrily. "I have a right
to the book, more than you or any other Bulking. I know
how to read the secret language. I can discover the truth of
the escape from the Weeuns."

"Let me have it," she said softly, wheedlingly. She leaned forward, bending closer to Merrily. "You can come here whenever you like, and I will read to you what Royal Bugle says, the very words he set down for every Bulking to remember."

Merrily looked uncertainly at Raymond. Raymond knew Wicker Bugle was right. They couldn't read the book, and it *had* belonged to her great-great. But still, they had found the book and by rights . . .

"Give it to her," he said quickly to Merrily.

Wicker Bugle smiled, an inward, satisfied smile.

"We will come here to hear what Royal Bugle said. How long will it take you to read the secret language?"

But Wicker Bugle's attention was only for the last book of Royal Bugle. She carefully loosened the drawstrings and drew out the aged, leather-bound book. She stroked the stained cover before she opened it.

"How I have longed for this last, great book," she said in a throaty voice. There were tears on her lined cheeks.

Wicker Bugle looked hungrily at the tiny, close writing. She touched the secret words lightly with a forefinger. She turned a few more pages, looking at the drawings, murmuring over their details. The others waited silently until she finally turned to the last page with its shaky signature: Royal Bugle.

Only then did she turn again to her visitors. "The first part is in a secret language I already know, and the third part is somewhat similar, but the middle and last parts have been changed by Royal Bugle. They will take me longer to read." She frowned. "I will be quick . . . I feel that time is running out fast, that we must learn the secrets of the Gartergates and the Finders soon, before . . ."

Wicker Bugle stood and began to stride around her garden with the book clasped in her long arms and her head down. Her voice grew louder and louder.

"The fools. They are like babies. Stupidly letting themselves be stalked and destroyed. They turn from the Finders, caring only for celebration and the eating of sweetcakes. The Finders warned them. The Gartergates . . . The Gartergates . . ."

Raymond stood up quietly and beckoned for Merrily and Bort to follow him.

Just as they reached the door into her plant-covered home, Wicker Bugle realized they were leaving.

"Where are you going?" she demanded. "Are you deserting the Finders, too? Leaving when you're needed the most?"

"Thank you for the lunch," Raymond told her, trying to make his voice as normal as possible. "We have to leave. Tonight is the Majester's party for his new house, and our parents expect us to go. Everyone is expected to go."

"Everyone?" Wicker Bugle snorted. "Not quite everyone. I wasn't invited."

Raymond didn't know what to say. It was no surprise that the Majester hadn't invited Wicker Bugle.

"But I'm sure you'd be welcome if you came," Merrily said from behind him.

"Not likely. Who wants to hear what this crazy old haggie has to say? No one ever wants to hear the truth."

"Thank you again," Raymond said hastily.

Wicker Bugle held up the last book.

"I thank you," she said solemnly and hugged the book to her. "Come. Let me show you the path back to Waterpushin."

They followed her through the cool little house and out her front door. Wicker Bugle pointed to a path through the tall trees.

"There you are," she said. "You're much closer to Waterpushin than you realize. This path will take you close to the Waterpush and past Gos's houseboat. Hurry home for your party, now."

Raymond, Merrily and Bort walked briskly down the clearly worn path. Raymond suddenly remembered he'd left Glom Gloom's crooky-staff leaning against the wall in Wicker Bugle's house. He turned and saw Wicker Bugle still standing and watching them, the book of her great-great held tightly in her arms.

He turned back and continued down the path. The crooky-staff would have to wait. He couldn't be going back and dealing with that crazy old haggie again this day.

* * *

JUST AFTER DARK, the long stream of guests began climbing Majester's Hill to the party. The Majester had put up lights on poles every few lengths along the path from the village to the top of Majester's Hill. There were also lights hanging from the fence Gos had built and lights on tall poles in the new gardens.

Raymond walked behind his parents, pretending he wasn't with them. Around him he could hear bits of conversation:

"I heard tell that there will be more food than anyone has ever seen in one place."

"Aye. All the bakers and cooks in Waterpushin have been heating their ovens and pulling out delicious morsels for days."

104

"I'm glad I haven't eaten all day."

"My Warren said the house even has a room just for the Majester's wife's fine dishes. And he should know; he helped build the house."

". . . never finer in all our seasons "

The air was taut with excitement. Behind Raymond, a group of little graders broke into a song, making up the words as they walked along:

> *To the Majester's house*
> *On Majester's Hill*
> *We'll play fine games*
> *And eat our fill*
> *Of sweets and cakes and popsies*
> *At the Majester's house*
> *Welcome, welcome, welcome.*

"Listen! There are musicians playing inside!"

Unmistakably, flowing from the open windows were the happy notes of "Wish on the Singing Turtle." There had never before been a house in Waterpushin big enough for the Waterpushin Musicmakers to play inside.

In the house, the music was louder, but it didn't cover the "ooh's" and "aaah's" as the Bulkings surveyed the wonders of the Majester's new house.

Off to one side of the front door was the great room where the musicians were playing. It was painted a dazzling white. Carved curly-vines and flowers wound their way up the corners of the walls and around the ceiling.

Off the great room was another room filled with tables and tables of food: crisp fruits and vegetables, tiny shaped breads and biscuits, plates and plates of sweetcakes, sweets and popsies. All arranged like jewels. Trays and trays and

105

bowls and platters. There was even more food than on Gloom Day.

Near the musicians was a long table covered with gifts from the Bulkings to the Majester and his family. There were bright jars of jell and hooked pan holders and lovely little things to look at. Raymond saw a Tiny that had to have been made by Gos. It was the Majester's new house, sitting high atop Majester's Hill. The picture was correct, but the house was too big, the door a trifle too ornate, the fence too imposing.

Other Bulkings were looking at the gifts on the tables, and Raymond heard murmurs:

"Oh, dear. I didn't know we were expected to bring gifts."

"What will the Majester think of me?"

Raymond saw Merrily laughing with Trillia Trader, the Majester's daughter. Merrily was wearing a dress with long sleeves, hiding her cut arm. Whatever had been in the ointment that Wicker Bugle had given him for the swelling above his eye had worked. There was only a slight mark, like a dirt smudge.

While Raymond was filling a plate with food, Bort stepped up beside him. His hair was all shiny and combed back from his face.

"I have to help my father tomorrow, so I won't be able to get away," he said softly. "Are you planning on going?"

Raymond wanted to go alone. He wanted to be the first to climb the Gartergates, the first to see what lay on the other side.

"I have much to do also," Raymond said, hoping Bort would think he meant he had much to do at home.

Bort nodded. "Perhaps the day after."

Raymond walked toward the great room, his plate heaped with sweetcakes and delicate, fragrant bits of food.

"Oh my!"

"Look out!"

"Careful!"

Raymond turned to see Bort on his knees on the floor with his plate of food scattering under the feet of the Bulkings.

Cakes and sweets rolled in every direction, smearing sugar frosting across the floor.

"Oooh," someone said as they stepped squarely onto a sweetcake.

A helping-woman was beside Bort immediately, lifting him to his feet, wiping off his clothes, picking up the spilled food. Bort's face was bright red.

Raymond's eyes met those of Gillus, who stood a length behind Bort, eating a sweetcake, a wide smile of amusement on his face.

In the great room, the Majester's wife was talking to Teacher Joiner near the table of gifts. Raymond pretended to look at the gifts so he could hear what they were saying.

". . . such a surprise, and in a new, well-built house like this," Teacher Joiner was saying.

Raymond picked up a delicately carved wooden tweakbird and inspected its wings.

"I know," the Majester's wife said, nodding so her silver ear baubles made tiny ringing sounds. "but that's how it is. There are definitely mouselings in the house. I don't know how they managed to get inside, but I heard them last night, scrabbling in the rooms after we were in bed. Trillia woke in the night, dreaming one had pulled her hair. But how could a mouseling do that? The little rascals somehow got into a plate of sweetcakes and ate nearly all of them."

107

Teacher Joined shook his head in sympathy. "Mouselings are a bother."

Raymond began to move away when he heard the Majester's wife ask, "Have you learned anything more about the missing map?"

He stopped, his heart pounding.

"We have a few clues," said Teacher Joiner. He puffed out his chest. "I am now on the Search and Find team, so I expect we'll discover who took it in no time."

"I expect so," she agreed. "Can you tell me about the clues?"

"Well, I'm not at liberty to say," Teacher Joiner said, "but since you're the Majester's wife, I can tell you this much: There's a young person who saw something the night the map disappeared and might be willing to come forward."

Raymond stood in disbelief. Not Bort or Merrily? Had they tricked him after all, then? He couldn't believe that. They were now as involved as he was. But who else was there who might have seen him?

"Do you like my carving of the tweak-bird?" Gillus asked, picking up the figure from the table and holding it out toward Raymond.

"It's very good."

"Thank you," Gillus replied and stroked the wooden wings. "I like to carve. Perhaps someday I'll carve you a rabbit."

Raymond said nothing.

"Have you had good luck hunting rabbits lately?" Gillus asked.

"I haven't been hunting."

"That's interesting. I was sure I saw you in the Wild Hills today."

"I was just out for a walk."

"You and Bort and Merrily Cumbers," Gillis taunted. "What an interesting threesome."

"It's not your concern," Raymond said and took a step away from Gillus.

"Raymond," Gillus said after him. His voice was soft.

Raymond turned around. Gillus replaced the tweak-bird on the gift table.

"If you three plan on taking walks in the forests, don't you think you might do better if you carried a *map?*"

Gillus laughed, and then hissed, "I *know.*"

Raymond watched Gillus turn and walk into the crowd of Bulkings in front of the musicians, his stomach sick.

14 · In the Tunnel

RAYMOND hurried through the forest, glancing at the stone markers and at Bort's slices in the trees, reassuring himself that he was on the right path to the Gartergates.

If Gillus was going to tell, there would be trouble. He wasn't afraid of the trouble as much as he was of being caught before he had a chance to see what was on the other side of the Gartergates.

The morning was already hot, and the mountains were blue in Warm Day haze. Even the nights were too warm for the dew to form on the grass.

As he walked, he surprised two deer cropping on shaded green grass. They bounded away, reminding him of Wicker Bugle's deer.

Had she read Royal Bugle's last book yet? Wilder Fibbey had been impatient and distruthful, Royal Bugle had said. But if that were for true, how had he saved the other Bulkings' lives? He wanted to believe his great-great was a true hero, a friend of the great Glom Gloom.

In the meadow before the tunnel that led to the Gartergates, Raymond paused and peered down the gloomy length. He wished the tunnel were shorter or lighter, or even that the trees were not so close to the cliff.

He forced himself to walk slowly, pushing the branches carefully out of his way. If he hurried, he knew panic would overtake him and he would run in fright down its length.

There was silence in the tunnel. His footsteps were muffled on the mossy floor, and the branches made no noise as he carefully held them back until he'd passed. He fought the need to look behind him, telling himself he was being foolish; nothing was behind him. Nevertheless, he longed for the too-hot sun and the bright light of the open meadow by the Gartergates.

As the way curved slightly, he saw several small animals in the tunnel in front of him. He couldn't tell what they were in the shadows. Bigger than rabbits, not big enough for deer. They froze as they became aware of Raymond's presence. He slowed his walk and then stopped altogether.

The animals didn't look right. They weren't on four feet; they walked upright on two feet!

All the figures but one jumped into the thick forest. They made hurrying, scrabbling noises as they pushed through the dense brush. The remaining figure stood as still as one of the statues in the Majester's new garden.

Raymond stood as motionless as the tiny figure, watching and waiting. His slinger was in his bag across his shoulder. Did he dare try to get it?

Slowly, carefully, he slipped his bag from his shoulder to his arm. When the strings were at his elbow, the small figure took a step forward, and in a slanting shaft of light through the trees, Raymond could make it out.

It was a Weeun.

It was small, so small Raymond couldn't believe it. It might come up just past his knee. Its dark clothing fit over its body in one piece, and a brown cap covered its head, but didn't hide a tangle of hair that showed bright red, even in the gloomy tunnel. Its eyes were as round as circles, and its nose turned up so much that Raymond could see its nostrils. Its mouth was round like its eyes.

The Weeun took a step forward. Raymond didn't move.

The Weeun put up a tiny hand.

"Hee-lo?" it said in a scratchy low voice.

The deep voice of the Weeun was like the sound of rocks grating together. There was no warmth in the voice, just hard, hard sounds that shot through Raymond like warning sounds before a terrible danger.

He shifted his weight slightly, wanting to turn and run. Fear prickled down his body, urging him to get away. His mouth was too dry to swallow.

"Hee-lo?" it said again, still holding up its hand.

Hee-lo? Was it saying, "hello"? Was the Weeun trying to talk to him?

Raymond felt a sharp pain in his arm. A tiny stick was imbedded in his skin. Another stick whizzed by his forehead and still another struck his cloth bag and fell to the ground.

The Weeun in the tunnel began shouting into the forest in the fearful, grating voice, using words Raymond couldn't understand. The voice was unbearable. It did more than touch his ears. It cut through his whole mind, blocking out all but his fear.

It was a trick. Raymond turned and ran back down the tunnel as another, and then another, of the tiny sticks flew past him. He paid no heed to the slapping bushes; he crashed against the side of the cliff; he tripped once and sprawled headlong against the bushes on the other wall of the tunnel, scraping his arms. But he went on.

112

When he broke through the tunnel into the meadow, he turned around to see if the Weeuns had followed him with their wicked sticks.

But the tunnel was as dark and gloomy and silent as when he'd entered it. The only sound was his panting breath. The Weeuns were in there, hiding and waiting in the darkness.

Raymond pulled the pointed stick out of his arm. Proof. It was proof that the Weeuns had invaded Waterpushin. They had broken through the Garter-gates.

Just as Wicker Bugle had said: Waterpushin was in danger. They were all in danger.

Raymond turned and hurried across the meadow. There was no more time. No more time.

The Majester. The Majester's house was the first house he'd come to. He would stop and tell the Majester. He would have to believe Raymond when he saw the sharp stick of the Weeuns.

Then he stopped, remembering the Majester's wife telling Teacher Joiner about the mouselings, describing their "scrabblings." Hadn't that been the way Wicker Bugle had described her feelings of foreboding: as "scrabblings in the night"? And Trillia had thought a mouseling had pulled her hair!

Raymond began to run again and soon felt hot streams of sweat sliding down his back, tasting the salt as sweat trickled from his forehead to his mouth. His chest hurt, and his cloth bag bounced against his back with every step.

Were the Weeuns still in the tunnel? Were they following him to Waterpushin? They were so small they could find secret ways into the village before the Bulkings even knew they were there.

The Majester's house stood cool and stately. The tall metal gates were closed. Raymond pulled the bell rope as hard as he could and shouted.

"Hurry, hurry! Where's the Majester?"

"Here, here, now. Stop that."

It was the doorman who had held the front door open for the party.

"I have to see the Majester at once," Raymond told him.

The doorman stood on the other side of the gate, not moving to unlock it.

"Now what can be so important as to cause all this excitement?" he asked calmly, eyeing Raymond with distrust.

"The Wee—. I can't tell you. I have to tell the Majester himself. Where is he?"

The doorman sniffed and looked at Raymond's streaked and sweaty face, his soiled clothes.

"I doubt if he'd want to see you in your condition. But no matter, he's not here."

"Where is he? I have to find him."

"He's in the village tending to the map-stealer."

Raymond stared at the doorman. Merrily. Bort. Gillus had told. He hadn't warned them, and it was his fault they'd been caught. All his fault.

"How did they catch them?" he asked.

The doorman looked at him sharply. "Them? There's only one that I know of, and no surprise, she is."

She? Merrily?

"Who?" Raymond shouted at the calm doorman.

The doorman threw up his arms.

"No need to scream. That crazy old haggie, Wicker Bugle. I always said she was a strange one. Can you . . ."

But Raymond was gone, running down the hill to Waterpushin, the sharp stick of the Weeuns held tightly in his hand.

15 · The Escape

THERE WERE groups of Bulkings standing and talking together on the Mid-cobbie. Some turned to stare at Raymond as he rushed past. They shook their heads when they saw his dirty face and clothes, his scraped arms and torn pants.

"Where's the Majester?" he called to two Fish Barrelers talking with the hat shopkeeper.

"At the Majester's old house. What . . . ."

Raymond hurried on. He heard the voices of many Bulkings before he even turned the corner to the square. Why were they at the Majester's old house? The house was empty now that Majester Trader and his family had moved to Majester's Hill.

"Raymond!"

It was Bort and Merrily, running to catch up with him.

"Where have you been? We've been looking everywhere for you. The Search and Find team has locked Wicker Bugle in the Majester's old house. Gillus told the Search and Find team that—"

"I went to the Gartergates," Raymond cut Merrily off. He held up the sharp stick that had been shot into his arm.

"The Weeuns . . . They've come through the Gartergates. They shot these at me in the tunnel. We have to tell the Majester. They have to be stopped."

Raymond started for the Majester's old house. "Where is he? We have to warn him."

Both Bort and Merrily gripped Raymond's arms.

"Wait," Bort said. "The Majester is just getting ready to give a speech in the square. Wicker Bugle wants to see us, especially you. At once. Before anything else is done."

"How can we see her if she's locked in the Majester's old house?"

"She's in a room that has a window into the back garden. We saw her just long enough for her to tell us to find you. Gillus told the Search and Find team that she had taken the map."

"Has she told who did take it?"

"Of course not," Merrily said indignantly. "She is loyal to our friendship."

Raymond couldn't feel so sure about Wicker Bugle. He held up the sharp stick again.

"But the Weeuns . . ."

"Wicker Bugle will know what to do," Bort said and led the way toward the Majester's old house.

There was a crowd gathered in the square, and still more Bulkings were entering the square to hear what the Majester would say.

"Wicker Bugle . . ."

". . . the precious map . . ."

"Will there be a punishing . . ."

"Who can remember a time . . ."

No one paid any attention to them as they approached the Majester's old house and slipped through the shrubs to the back garden.

Wicker Bugle sat in a chair by a high, open window, her eyes peering sharply as she waited.

"You found him," she said when she saw Raymond.

Raymond stepped up to the window.

"The Weeuns, Wicker Bugle. I saw the Weeuns in the tunnel. They shot at me with sharp sticks." He held up the sharp stick. "They've come through the Gartergates! We have to tell the Majester. We have to stop them."

Wicker Bugle looked at him without a change of expression. Hadn't she heard him? Didn't she understand what he was saying?

"The Weeuns, Wicker Bugle," he said, louder.

"Quiet," Bort warned, glancing about the garden.

"I thought they had already come through," Wicker Bugle said calmly. "I have to have Royal Bugle's last book. I must finish reading it."

"Now?" Raymond asked. "It can wait. The Weeuns are in Waterpushin. They may already be preparing to attack."

Wicker Bugle shook her head. "My great-great says the Weeuns are not honest enough to attack in daylight. They wait until darkness or until they find Bulkings in close places."

The tunnel had been gloomy-dark. Majester Trader's wife had heard the scrabbling noises at night.

Wicker Bugle stood up. "Get me out of here, now," she commanded. "We can't know how to save Waterpushin until I've finished reading Royal Bugle's last book."

Raymond put the pointed Weeun stick in his bag and knelt on his hands and knees under the window. Bort and Merrily helped Wicker Bugle step over the sill onto Raymond's back. She stepped lightly to the ground.

The Majester hadn't thought of a guard for Wicker Bugle. The rules of Waterpushin were enough. Who would ever think of escaping if they were told not to?

Wicker Bugle straightened her flappy clothes and

pushed her gray hair back from her eyes. She smiled grimly at Raymond, Bort and Merrily.

"We must go to my house immediately. It may already be too late."

Merrily touched Wicker Bugle's arm lightly, glancing quickly about the gardens.

"Let's go this way," Merrily said and led them through the back gardens onto a narrow wynd.

Behind them they could hear bits of the Majester's speech to the crowd in the square.

". . . never in our gentle history . . . grave problem of what we should do . . . you all know Wicker . . ."

They were nearly out of Waterpushin, nearly to the Waterpush River where Gos's houseboat was tied. Only a short way past Gos's houseboat the path began that would take them through the Wild Hills to Wicker Bugle's house.

A Bulking child with a red popsie in her mouth stood in the wynd facing the four of them, her face smeared with popsie juice and dirt. They were close, so close to the path. Safety was within sight.

Merrily smiled at the child and said, "Hello. Is that a good popsie?"

The child nodded and held up the popsie to Merrily.

With her smile stiff, Merrily said brightly, "No thank you. It's yours."

Then the child pointed the popsie at Wicker Bugle and gravely looked at the tall, thin figure.

"Wicker Bugle," she said.

Merrily looked wildly at Raymond, then smiled and asked, "Do you have a doll?"

"Wicker Bugle, Wicker Bugle," the child singsonged louder and louder.

A door slammed and a voice called, "Lucy, Lucy. Where are you?"

"Wicker Bugle, Wicker Bugle," she still singsonged, jumping from one foot to the other, waving her popsie.

"Let's be gone from here," Wicker Bugle said and began to run.

They ran uncaringly toward the Waterpush River, past Gos's houseboat, where the waters gently nosed against the old wood, and up the little rise onto the path into the Wild Hills.

Wicker Bugle stopped and leaned against a tree stump, her hand against her chest and her face red.

"Are you all right?" Bort asked.

"Aye," Wicker Bugle gasped and stood up straight. "Let's be going."

She strode ahead of them to her home, her step firm but her thin shoulders rising and falling.

"We're too late," Wicker Bugle cried.

They stood in front of Wicker Bugle's underground house. The nearly invisible door was standing open. A bench and plant were lying on the ground beside it, the pot smashed and the flower broken and twisted in its scattered earth.

"The Weeuns?" Raymond asked, looking for signs of the tiny creatures.

"Gillus," Wicker Bugle said. "If he took the book, we're lost, all of Waterpushin is lost."

Her home was in tatters. Books were pulled from their shelves and stacks of books were knocked over. They lay open and tumbled on the floor, all over the room. The table was on its side and food was scattered about the floor. Every shelf and cupboard was bare, its contents on the floor. Even

Wicker Bugle's bed had been pulled apart and the blankets thrown to the floor.

"Gillus?" Bort asked. "What was he looking for?"

"Ooooh," Wicker Bugle moaned, her voice catching as she looked about her jumbled house. She dropped to her knees and began going through the scattered books.

"The last book. Treasure," she said.

"Treasure?"

"Help me look," Wicker Bugle said. "Find the last book. It's got to be here. If only he didn't take it."

They began sorting through the books, placing the ones they'd already looked through in straight little stacks beside Wicker Bugle's bed.

Wicker Bugle threw her belongings haphazardly about her room as she looked for the book, muttering to herself, "It has to be here. It has to be."

They searched through every book and uncovered every bare space of floor, every shelf, even looking in the cooling cupboard in the floor. But the last book of Royal Bugle was not to be found.

Wicker Bugle sat on the floor in the middle of her disheveled house and began to cry. Merrily dropped to her knees beside her and put her arms around her. Wicker Bugle leaned her head against Merrily's shoulder and sobbed, her mouth open and her eyes squeezed tightly shut.

Raymond left the little house and went into the garden. He couldn't bear to see an adult Bulking's tears. He had only seen his mother cry once, and that had shocked him so much he hadn't been able to speak to her for days. It was like seeing a part of a Bulking that should never be seen. All much too private.

There were still plates and food on the table under the

tree from their lunch the day before. Had it actually been only the day before? Wicker Bugle must have gone directly to reading the last book without cleaning up their lunch. There were wingers on the plates, swarming over the dried up bits of food.

Gillus. What was he after? A treasure? What kind of treasure could there be?

The Weeuns might already be grouping in the tunnel, gathering in the dense forest that was too thick for the Bulkings to walk through. The four of them should be *doing* something, not just sitting in Wicker Bugle's house while she wept.

Raymond kicked at the leg of one of the benches. It wobbled, and something heavy fell from the bench to the grass.

It was the last book of Royal Bugle.

He picked it up and rushed back across the garden to Wicker Bugle's house.

"I found it!" Raymond shouted.

Wicker Bugle jumped up from Merrily's arms and ran to Raymond. She tore the book from his hands and began leafing through it.

Laughing aloud, she leaned over and kissed Raymond on the forehead.

"The map . . . he only took the map."

She held up the book and showed them where the page had been torn raggedly from the book.

"Now we know where he is, at least."

"Where who is?" Raymond asked.

"Gillus, of course," she answered, her brows drawn in a frown, her eyes moving hurriedly about her house.

Merrily stood up and asked, "What has Gillus done?"

But Wicker Bugle waved her hand at Merrily "Later, later. We must be on our way now."

She picked up two of her gray dresses from the floor and tied the sleeves and necks shut, turning them into rough bags.

"Here," she said "Put in food and blankets and candles."

She began stuffing another cloth bag with her personal belongings: strange little boxes, books, a tiny statue of a deer, two dresses. Lastly, she put in the book of Royal Bugle.

"They'll come here looking for me," she said sadly. "Perhaps nothing will be left when they discover I'm gone."

Wicker Bugle lifted the heavy bag to her shoulders. "We may have to hide from them until I have finished the last book and we have a plan."

"Are we going to hide in the Wild Hills?" Bort asked.

Wicker Bugle picked up Glom Gloom's crooky-staff, which was still leaning against her door sill, and gave it to Raymond.

"This is in your trust now, Raymond Fibbey," she said.

The crooky-staff's worn wood felt warm and sturdy; Glom Gloom had trusted its strength, and now Raymond would also trust it.

As they left the little house, Wicker Bugle answered Bort's question.

"Not in the Wild Hills," she said. "We're going to the Gartergates."

16 · Gillus

"*G*ILLUS came early this morning and demanded to know the way to the treasure," Wicker Bugle told them as they made their way into the forest.

"What treasure?" Raymond asked.

"I asked him also. He must have seen you three in the Wild Hills. He added that together with the missing map and my talk about the Gartergates and decided I was leading you to a treasure."

"Did he follow us to the Gartergates?" Bort asked.

"Only partway. Gillus may know the ways of potmending or fishing, but he doesn't know the ways of the forest." Wicker Bugle sighed. "But with the well-marked map from Royal Bugle's book, he's sure to find the Gartergates."

"When I told Gillus there was no treasure, he left, saying he'd get even with me. I never expected to open my door a short while later and see Teacher Joiner with the entire Search and Find team come to fetch me. They said a young witness had seen me take the map from Gimly School. Of course I knew who had told them that."

Raymond squirmed uncomfortably inside, thinking of the map under his bed.

"You could have told them who had really taken the map," he said.

Wicker Bugle turned and glared at Raymond.

"Don't be a fool," she said curtly.

Raymond felt his face flush hot.

Gillus. Gillus was the cause of it all: the tumbled house, turning them into outlaws when they should be telling the Majester about the Weeuns and making a plan to save Waterpushin.

"Imagine," Wicker Bugle mused, "an entire Search and Find team to take one harmless old lady back to Waterpushin. It's been out of memory since there's been a crime in Waterpushin, and they didn't know what to do with me. What would they have done if the Majester's old house hadn't been empty?"

"Gillus must have gone back to your house after they'd taken you away," Merrily said.

"Aye," said Wicker Bugle. "I was reading the last book of Royal Bugle when Gillus came. I tried·to hide it from his eyes, and he must have thought that's where the clues to the treasure were. The map would have been the only thing he could understand."

Raymond suddenly stopped and dropped his bags to the ground.

"Wait!"

Merrily, Bort and Wicker Bugle stopped and turned to look at Raymond.

"Do you mean to say," he said to Wicker Bugle, "that we are on our way to the Gartergates, knowing that the Weeuns have entered Waterpushin, knowing we could be in terrible danger . . . we are going to the Gartergates to find *Gillus?*" Raymond sputtered in his anger. "Gillus! Gillus is the one who betrayed you, Wicker Bugle! He lied and ruined your home. He bedevils Bort. He took apart Bort's father's wagon, and who knows what else."

125

Bort looked sharply at Raymond.

"And now we are going to put ourselves in danger for *Gillus?*" he finished.

Wicker Bugle wiped the sweat from her face onto the sleeve of her dress.

"Gillus is a troublemaker. He's not been honorable," Wicker Bugle said, combing her fingers through her rough hair. "But, Raymond. Mayhap this be hard for you to understand, but Gillus is Gos's charge. And Gos is my friend. If I had a child in trouble and Gos could help, I know he would be the first Bulking to my aid."

"Then why didn't we stop and tell Gos?"

"We were in danger of being found out, remember?" Merrily reminded him.

"And I didn't know yet what Gillus had done," Wicker Bugle finished.

"So let's go back and tell Gos now," Raymond said.

Merrily twisted her yellow hair, and Bort looked away.

"There is no time, Raymond," Wicker Bugle said. "If the Weeuns are through the Gartergates, as you say, then Gillus is in grave danger.

"I must hide until the last book is finished. Who could ever find us at the Gartergates? Don't be forgetting that it will be known who helped me escape. We are all in need of hiding until we have more proof. When we have found Gillus and I've discovered the secrets the Finders used to defeat the Weeuns, then we will return to Waterpushin and tell the Majester."

"I still have the sharp stick the Weeuns shot at me," Raymond said.

"Is that enough proof?" Wicker Bugle asked. "Does it look any different from a stick you might have sharpened yourself? Asides," she added gently, "are you always to be believed?"

Raymond turned his back on them. Distruthful, Royal Bugle had called his great-great, Wilder Fibbey.

"Raymond."

It was Bort.

"Do you think Wicker Bugle could find Gillus and convince him of his danger by herself?"

He thought of the unpredictable, emotional Wicker Bugle and the suspicious, sly Gillus.

"Probably not,"

"Wicker Bugle has been loyal to our short friendship. She could have told where the map is. If the Search and Find team had gone to your house, they would have found the map."

Bort was right. Raymond would have walked unknowingly into Waterpushin to tell the Majester of the Weeuns, and the Search and Find team would have been waiting for him. They wouldn't have believed him about the Weeuns. They would have thought it was just an excuse, an attempt to stay out of trouble.

Raymond picked up his bags and threw them over his shoulders. He stepped between Merrily and Wicker Bugle and said gruffly, "We'd best be hurrying if we're going to find Gillus before he causes more trouble."

Wicker Bugle smiled, and Merrily touched Raymond's arm lightly before she picked up her bag.

As they walked, Wicker Bugle told them what she had learned from Royal Bugle's last book.

"There is a door at the back of the hollow in the Gartergates," she said, "where you found the book and spyglass and Glom Gloom's crooky-staff."

"I didn't see a door," Bort said, "and I was inside the hollow."

"Royal Bugle himself made the door," Wicker Bugle said proudly. "It is made to be invisible on the other side of the Gartergates, to form a tight seal. It can only be opened from this side. Glom Gloom wanted a door so the Bulkings could be assured the other side of the Gartergates was safe."

"Royal Bugle told of sneaking among the Bulking slaves and helping a few Bulkings come with the Finders to Waterpushin to prepare the village and begin building the Gartergates. Then Royal Bugle changed the secret language. I felt I was close to learning how to read it when Gillus came. That is all I know now. But I was so close to reading it, so close . . ."

They paused to rest in the little meadow by the entrance to the tunnel.

"I was almost through the tunnel when I saw them," Raymond said.

The tiny meadow and surrounding forest seemed to wait innocently in the bright sunshine. A tweak-bird sang happily from a tree behind them, and the meadow buzzed with wingers dancing about each other. But Raymond didn't trust to the way things seemed. Even now, the Weeuns could be hiding in the dark forest, watching them, waiting to attack.

"Bort, you go first with your sharp eyes," Wicker Bugle finally said, straightening her shoulders. "I will come behind you. Merrily, you stay close behind me, and Raymond, you follow last and keep an eye over your shoulder."

The tunnel was lighter than it had been earlier in the morning. A little sunlight filtered through the branches overhead. They walked slowly and carefully, each of them peering in front of them and into the dense forest.

Once, Raymond bumped the awkward crooky-staff against the cliff as he was turning to look behind him.

"Thwunk," it sounded in the stillness, and they all gasped.

"Sorry," Raymond whispered when he saw the three white faces staring back at him.

There was no movement in the stillness. No scrabbling noises to their side. No sharp sticks appearing mysteriously from the forest.

The hot Warm Day sun struck them, and they were through the tunnel. Unharmed, safe.

Wicker Bugle dropped her bag to the ground and stretched her weary arms. She looked up at the Gartergates.

"Oh, Good Gloom," she said.

Gillus was on the Gartergates. He had made his way up to the opening of the hollow and was clinging to the side of the rocks with his head and shoulders inside the hollow. They could tell from the way his shoulders were working that he was feeling the insides of the dark hollow. Searching for treasure.

"Gillus!" Raymond shouted.

"Don't frighten him!" Bort said. "He'll fall."

Gillus jerked when he heard Raymond call his name, but instead of falling, in a kind of pulling jump he entered the small confines of the hollow.

Wicker Bugle ran to the foot of the Gartergates.

"Come down, Gillus. There's no treasure."

"Hah!" came Gillus's muffled voice from inside the hollow. "I don't believe you."

"For true, Gillus," Merrily called up to him. "We swear it."

Gillus pulled his feet into the hollow after him.

"If there's no treasure, what's this door for?" his voice came down to them.

"Don't open it!" Wicker Bugle shouted, her voice fierce.

"So this is the door to the treasure, then, is it?"

"We've got to stop him," Bort said and began to climb up toward the hollow. But it went slowly, his hands and feet searching for every hold.

There was silence from the hollow; then they heard "Oh no," followed by a muffled shout. Then silence.

"What happened?" Merrily whispered.

Raymond shrugged helplessly. Bort was still making his way to the opening of the hollow. There seemed to be light there, perhaps coming from the other side.

"Careful, careful," Wicker Bugle said softly, and Raymond's hand tightened white on the crooky-staff.

Bort pulled himself into the hollow. None of them moved during the long, silent wait. They stared at the hole in the Gartergates that seemed to have swallowed both Gillus and Bort.

Then the light was gone from the entrance to the hollow, and Bort's feet and legs emerged. He turned and slid down the Gartergates.

Wicker Bugle was the first to reach him. His eyes were wide in his white face, and his entire body was shaking.

"It's all right, Bort," Wicker Bugle said and put her arm around his shoulders. "Just rest quietly."

"Gillus is gone," Bort said in a gasp.

"Gone?" Merrily repeated.

"The Weeuns?" Wicker Bugle asked.

"He must have fallen from the hollow because the door's too high for the Weeuns to reach," Bort said.

"The Weeuns probably never knew of the door before," Wicker Bugle told them. "My great-great was too skilled a craftsman."

"What are the Weeuns doing with Gillus?" Raymond asked.

Bort trembled, and Wicker Bugle tightened her arm around him and soothed, "It's all right. All is well."

"There were Weeuns everywhere. I don't know what they were doing before Gillus fell, but they had ropes and pointed sticks. Gillus was lying at the bottom of the Garter-gates, stunned. They were on him before he could move."

"Did they see you?"

Bort nodded. "They threw their pointed sticks at me, but they couldn't throw high enough. I saw Weeuns standing by an opening in the ground as if they were guarding it."

"An underground passage!" Raymond said. "That's how they got into Waterpushin: under, not over the Garter-gates!"

They glanced about them, searching the meadow for signs of an opening to the underground passage.

"It wouldn't be here," Wicker Bugle said. "It must be in the densest part of the forest."

"I saw tiny houses," Bort continued. "Row after row after row. Gray tiny houses and narrow wynds and cobbies.

"And everywhere were the Weeuns. Weeun mothers and their Weeun children. Weeun men and women. Weeuns sitting by the cobbies and wynds, doing nothing, just sitting. Weeun children playing and fighting and running together, with no clothes on in the heat.

"There were no brightly colored houses. No bright clothes. No flowers. The grass was brown. There were no big trees as we have in Waterpushin; only low bushes, and the leaves on those were withered and dull."

"What color hair did they have?" Raymond asked, thinking of the red-haired Weeun in the tunnel.

"Everyone but the children wore caps. The children mostly had dull brown hair. Their hair grows down their foreheads almost to their eyes."

"Will they harm Gillus?" Merrily asked, but there could be no answer.

Wicker Bugle stood up in her usual abrupt flurry of movements.

"I must read the last book now. We have to learn the Finders' secret to defeating the Weeuns. Then perhaps we will know how to free Gillus."

"Free Gillus!" Raymond exploded. "He got himself into his own trouble. How can we possibly free him from the Weeuns?"

The others were silent.

"It's Waterpushin we have to save," he said, trying to explain, angry at the shame he felt over their silence. "If we try to save Gillus now, we may lose Waterpushin. How can we save Gillus when he's already in the hands of the Weeuns?"

"It's not the Bulking way," Merrily reminded him. "No matter what Gillus may have done, Bulkings must keep faith with each other."

"The Finders were our great-greats," she continued. "Maybe they had no great fondness for the Bulkings they led through the Gartergates to Waterpushin, either. But they risked their lives to bring them here, to make Waterpushin safe against the Weeuns. The Finders didn't abandon the enslaved Bulkings, even though those same Bulkings had forced them to live separately.

"I'm frightened. But I think the Finders must have been frightened, too."

132

Raymond hadn't thought of the Finders as being frightened. They had been heroes, special Bulkings, not ordinary and small like him and Bort and Merrily.

"You are strong and brave, Raymond, and we need you. You must do your great-great proud. As we all must do."

Wicker Bugle was sitting against a tree near their bags. She held Royal Bugle's last book on her lap and was frowning and mumbling over it.

Something special had come down to Merrily and Bort and Raymond from their great-greats. Something special to Wicker Bugle, too.

And now they four were together, the only Bulkings who believed the old stories and who might be able to save Gillus and Waterpushin from the Weeuns.

Raymond walked slowly around the meadow, thinking of what Merrily had said. He used the crooky-staff like a walking stick, matching it to each step he took.

17 · Bort's Decision

ON THE LATE afternoon they opened the bags they'd brought from Wicker Bugle's house and set up a camp, then gathered sticks and wood to build a fire. Wicker Bugle paid no attention to what they were doing, but sat hunched over Royal Bugle's last book, her head bent low over the secret language.

They kept looking between the trees, but saw nothing. The forest was silent, a dark silence that rang in Raymond's ears. They had arranged their camp as close to the Gartergates as possible, and Raymond set the sticks for the fire between them and the meadow so they would all be together between the Gartergates and the fire.

"When it becomes dusky," Bort said as they sat by the unlit fire, "I'm going to go back into the hollow and open the door to see what's happening on the other side."

Raymond felt admiration for Bort. Merrily was right; they were frightened, but they must do what need be done.

He nodded to Bort. "That's a good idea."

"I'll take the spyglass with me. I didn't think to use it the first time I looked through the door." He shrugged. "I suppose I was too frightened."

"We were all frightened," Merrily said.

Bort took the spyglass from inside his tunic, slipped it out of its cloth bag and held it out.

"B. D. Gard," he said solemnly. "Bartholomew Dare Gard."

"One of the Finders," Merrily said, just as solemnly.

"A great, great Bulking," Raymond added. "He would have been proud."

The sun soon slipped behind the trees, and the dense forest made long shadows across the meadow.

"I'll start the fire now," Raymond said.

Merrily began lifting the jars and packages from the store of food to see what they held. It was a strange assortment: jells and paturnies and bread and odd little pickles that Wicker Bugle must have made. Merrily spread jell on bread. Then she opened a jar of spicy porridge and poured it in one of the pots to heat on the fire.

As the porridge heated, they sat beside the cheerful little fire and told stories of school and Teacher Joiner, their laughter echoing in the meadow.

When the porridge was hot, Merrily took a bowl to Wicker Bugle, but she ignored it. Merrily left it on the ground beside her.

As soon as it became dusky, Bort sighed and stood up. He brushed his pants, straightened his tunic and touched the spot where the spyglass rested.

"I think I'm ready," he said and looked up at the Gartergates, to where the hole to the hollow stood out black against the gray stones.

"You must be very careful," Merrily told him, her hands pulling at her hair.

"I'm not sure how good we would be at rescuing two Bulkings," Raymond said, and Bort laughed, a laugh that sounded like a gargle.

Merrily and Raymond stood and watched Bort as he

climbed the Gartergates, a dark shadow against the darkening rock.

At the mouth of the hollow, Bort turned and waved down to them with one hand. Raymond clasped his hands together above his head in a Bulking sign of good luck.

Bort pulled himself inside the hollow. As his feet disappeared, Raymond felt a sudden loneliness. What if something should happen to Bort? He realized then how much he depended on Bort's quiet ways, his sharp eyes. Even his skinny, smallish stature was a comfort.

"What if . . ." Merrily began.

"Let's tell Wicker Bugle what Bort's done," Raymond said, not wanting to hear that she was feeling the same fears.

18 · What Bort Saw

ORT RESTED from his climb, lying on his stomach in the narrow hollow. It was too dark to see inside the hollow, and he glanced behind him, over his heels, at the reassuring dim light coming from the entrance.

He felt along the walls and ceiling of the hollow. They were smooth; great care had been taken in their building. He felt along the edges of what he knew to be the door. There was only a slight indentation in the smooth rock where the door fit into the Gartergates. The handle was made from a straight piece of heavy metal, bent at an angle so it had to be pulled down to open the door.

It moved smoothly, without a sound, as if it might have been hinged and oiled yesterday. Bort pushed it open just enough to be able to see into the land of the Weeuns. He looked down at the ground, at the foot of the Gartergates.

There was nothing there. No ugly little Weeuns waiting for him. He was safe.

To Bort's right were tall torches, blazing in front of an entrance into the ground—the underground passage that the Weeuns had used to enter Waterpushin. Two Weeuns stood in front of the entrance, holding lances. They were dressed in dark clothes and wore dark caps pulled down over their hair.

A third Weeun was approaching the two Weeuns, also carrying a lance. He was coming from the direction of the Gartergates, and Bort suspected he had been standing beneath the secret door in the Gartergates, waiting for some Bulking to do exactly what Bort was doing. If Bort had been earlier . . .

Bort watched the three guards for a long time to be sure they wouldn't look up and see him. But they paid no attention to the Gartergates. They talked together, and once Bort saw them pass around a bottle from which they each took long drinks.

Where was Gillus? Where could the tiny Weeuns hide a Bulking?

Bort removed the spyglass from his tunic and carefully opened the door wider and wider, until he could see all of the landscape in front of him. He sat at the edge of the door, his feet pulled inside, one hand on the door handle, the other holding the spy glass.

There were tiny figures milling in the cobbies and wynds. In the dusky light they all appeared as gray and dully dressed as Wicker Bugle. There were so many! So small, so gray and so sinister.

The Weeuns didn't walk like the Bulkings. When they stood, they stood straight; but when they walked or ran, they bent their bodies forward as if they were racing their feet to their destination.

With the spyglass to his eye, Bort looked at their faces. It was as if they were only a few lengths from him! He had to take the spyglass away to assure himself that the Weeuns were still in their own land.

The faces were nearly all the same: round, round eyes that didn't seem to blink. When Bort looked at their eyes, something made him want to keep staring. He remembered the hypnotism and forced himself to look away, determined not to look into their eyes again.

The hair on the Weeuns' heads grew almost down to their eyebrows, so bushy they needed the caps to keep it out of their eyes. Every nose on every face was short and turned up. The mouths under the noses were round, as round as the eyes. The Weeuns were all thin. Their cheek-bones stood out in their faces, and their arms and legs were like skinny sticks.

Bort saw that the Weeuns were gathering in the middle of their village. There was already a large crowd in an open square, and more were joining, jostling and elbowing each other. He thought he could hear the sounds of many voices. The harsh noises made his neck prickle.

Bort couldn't believe it when he saw two Weeun men take hold of a Weeun woman and shove her so roughly that she fell. No one in the crowd paid any attention, and though he kept his spyglass on the spot where the woman had fallen in the midst of the pushing crowd, Bort didn't see her get up again.

From another cobbie, a procession advanced on the crowded square. There was no mistaking that these Weeuns were different from the Weeuns in the crowd. These Weeuns were not thin like all the others, but looked well-fed and muscular. They carried shields and wicked barbed lances.

A double row of Weeuns led the procession. Behind them was another Weeun, obviously of great importance, maybe their king. He was almost fat. His roundness would have been comical if it hadn't been for his haughty, cruel expression.

In tight marching formation behind the Weeun king came more Weeuns, carrying shields and lances.

When the procession reached the Weeun square, the Weeuns in the crowd began to hastily make way. Those who were too slow were shoved with the shields, or poked by the lances of the marching Weeuns. Bort saw a Weeun holding his arm with a blood-covered hand.

When a way was cleared through the crowd, Bort saw what was in the center, what all the Weeuns were pushing and shoving and hurting each other to see.

It was Gillus.

Out of wood lashed together with ropes, the Weeuns had built a cage so small that Gillus was lying on his side with his knees drawn up to his chest. With the powerful spyglass, Bort could see Gillus's face, held trancelike, his eyes staring as he lay helpless, surrounded by Weeuns, unable to move.

How could they ever rescue Gillus when the Weeuns were holding him as a spectacle? Who knew what the Weeuns would do to Gillus. Bort was sure they could think of a hundred horrible things.

The procession halted in front of Gillus's cage, and the lance-carrying Weeuns formed a semicircle around the fat Weeun king and Gillus.

The crowd fell silent. The Weeuns waited attentively, all watching their king and Gillus.

The Weeun king walked around the cage, motioning for one of the soldiers to prod Gillus with his lance and then laughing as Gillus's eyes closed tightly.

Bort couldn't watch the cruelty. He turned the spyglass to the eager crowd.

To one side of the crowd Bort saw a Weeun standing on a bench under a street lamp. The Weeun's hair shone bright red in the light where it edged his cap. His heavy brows were pulled together, and his round mouth was pursed shut.

When the Weeun king raised his arms for attention and began to speak, the red-haired Weeun shook his head and got down from the bench. Bort lost him for a few moments and then found him again as he hurried up a cobbie away from the crowd. Where was he going? Every other Weeun was either in the crowd or hurrying to the square to have a look at Gillus. But Bort lost the red-haired Weeun among the close, dark houses.

Bort burned to help Gillus. No matter how deceitful and foolish Gillus had been, he did not deserve to be treated in such a way.

But what could he do? Bort took the spyglass from his eye and tried to make a mental picture of the land of the Weeuns: where the underground passage was located, the different routes to the square where Gillus was caged.

Then Bort smiled to himself. There was no need to remember the routes to the square. If he were standing in their land, his height would allow him to see the square from wherever he stood. The houses in the Weeun land couldn't be any higher than his shoulder, at most.

The guards at the entrance to the underground passage were looking down at the square where the crowd was gathered. Bort had seen no other Weeuns come near the underground passage. They were all too interested in their Bulking captive.

He carefully shut the door behind him, pushing against it several times to be sure it was secured.

19 · Miffit

ORT is in the hollow," Raymond said to Wicker Bugle.

Wicker Bugle still sat on the ground where she'd first dropped with Royal Bugle's last book. As the shadows deepened, she leaned closer and closer over the writing, mumbling and holding her head in frustration.

"He's going to open the door in the hollow and see what the Weeuns are doing with Gillus," Raymond said when she didn't answer.

"Mmm," Wicker Bugle murmured, but didn't look up.

Raymond returned to Merrily by the fire. She was looking up at the entrance to the hollow.

"I wish he'd come back," Merrily said, poking at the fire with a stick.

As the sky darkened, they moved closer to the fire. It would soon be totally dark, a darkness that would last about an hour before the moon came up. They would feel safer then.

Wicker Bugle came into the light of the fire, the last book in her hands. She rubbed at a cramp in her leg, sat down, and shook her head wearily.

"This secret language is the hardest of all to read. I know I will learn it, but will I learn it in time?"

"Would you like one of the candles?" Merrily asked.

"That would help, thank you."

Looking around the shadowy meadow, Wicker Bugle suddenly asked, "Where's Bort?"

"He's in the hollow, watching the Weeuns through the secret door," Raymond told her.

Wicker Bugle looked up at the Gartergates with longing.

"That was brave." She turned to stare thoughtfully into the fire. "If only I were younger. . . . The sights he must be seeing."

Raymond suddenly remembered that he had wanted to be the first to climb the Gartergates, to discover if the Weeuns were for true. That seemed long ago.

Bort stepped into the firelight, his hand over the spyglass in his tunic.

"Bort!" Merrily cried.

"I have seen Gillus," he said, and told them what he had observed: the thin Weeuns and the fat Weeun king; Gillus's cage and the tormentors; the underground passage, and the barren Weeun land.

"I saw more Weeuns in that square than there are Bulkings in all of Waterpushin."

Bort shuddered as he remembered the eager Weeuns in the crowd as Gillus was taunted and prodded.

"They are as horrible as the old stories say. Even the distant sound of their voices filled me with a dread so great it was all I could do to keep from closing the secret door and returning to Waterpushin."

Raymond nodded, remembering how the voice of the red-haired Weeun had affected him: a cold, icy fear.

"Will they attack us tonight?" Wicker Bugle asked.

"They'll be too busy with Gillus to come through the underground passage tonight," Bort said. "But we should keep guard."

"I can do it," Wicker Bugle said. "I'll be awake all night learning the secret language."

Raymond thought of Wicker Bugle's inattentiveness. The Weeuns could surround her, and she wouldn't notice, unless they sat on Royal Bugle's book itself.

"You shouldn't have to concentrate on anything but the last book," Raymond said to her. "Merrily, Bort and I will take turns watching."

"I can watch first," Merrily offered.

"I'll take my turn next," Bort said.

"And I'll take the last watch," Raymond said. "While we're watching, we can think of ways to rescue Gillus."

* * *

THE MOON was high when Bort woke Raymond for his turn at watching. The little meadow glimmered in the pale light.

"No sign of any Weeuns," Bort whispered as Raymond gave him his blanket. "Wicker Bugle finally fell asleep a short while ago. I put out her candle."

Wicker Bugle was slumped over the book, her hand still holding the pencil she had been using.

"Did she learn the secret language?" Raymond asked.

Bort shook his head. "Not yet."

Bort rolled up in the blanket on the ground, and Raymond stepped into the meadow, away from the glowing fire. The bright moon was directly overhead, and it turned his shadow into a small, dark spot beneath his feet. It was too bright for there to be any stars, but a few fluffy white clouds hung beneath the moon.

Raymond walked around the edge of the meadow, the crooky-staff moving naturally with his every step. He thought of Gillus as Bort had described him: at the mercy of the evil Weeuns, with no place to hide, no way to escape. They had to do something. Gillus was more than a lying trickster who had caused their trouble; he was a fellow Bulking. They were together, whether they wanted to be or not.

It was still a while until daylight. Raymond walked, afraid to sit down, afraid he'd fall asleep.

Something moved at the edge of the meadow. A deer? A Weeun? Raymond gripped the crooky-staff with both hands.

A small figure stepped from the forest and stood facing him. Raymond knew at once, even though he couldn't see the red hair, that this was the same Weeun he'd met in the tunnel. The Weeun who had tricked him.

Anger exploded inside him like a new twig fire, and he rushed toward the Weeun, his crooky-staff raised.

The Weeun didn't try to run back into the forest but held his empty hands in front of him.

"Nononono," he said.

Raymond stopped, the crooky-staff upraised, ready to bring it down upon the red-haired Weeun.

The small figure cringed; his eyes squeezed shut and his shoulders hunched, waiting for the crooky-staff to fall. His hands were still open in front of him.

Were there more Weeuns hiding in the shadowed forest? Should he shout and awaken the others? Raymond kept the crooky-staff ready, waiting for the sharp sticks from the forest, for some trickery from this single Weeun.

The Weeun opened one eye and cautiously looked up at Raymond. The sight of the moonlight reflecting from the Weeun's eye made a cold fear creep down Raymond's arms. His hands tightened on the crooky-staff.

The Weeun's other eye opened. The fear thickened, and Raymond forced himself to look away from the powerful eyes, into the forest for signs of other Weeuns, for any movement, any sound of treachery.

All was still and quiet. Wicker Bugle, Bort and Merrily slept on peacefully. The trees and bushes didn't move.

The Weeun said something. At the sound of its gravelly voice, Raymond felt once again that strange fear, the urge to run recklessly away from the sound. It was an evil, nightmare sound, a sound he couldn't awaken from and leave behind. He raised the crooky-staff higher, more threateningly. Was the Weeun giving orders to hidden friends?

Nothing happened. The Weeun cringed again, but he repeated what he had said.

"Sorey," it sounded like. Raymond didn't understand.

The Weeun slowly, carefully, pointed toward the tunnel.

"Sorey," he said again.

Raymond didn't dare to turn and look at the tunnel.

The Weeun pointed again toward the tunnel, his little finger poking into the air.

"Lass time. Sorey," the Weeun said.

The Weeun poked at himself with a finger, jabbing his arm.

"Hurt you lass time. Sorey," he said, shaking his capped head.

Finally Raymond understood what he was saying:

"Hurt you last time. Sorry." The Weeun was apologizing for the attack in the tunnel!

"Why?" he asked suspiciously.

The face of the Weeun seemed to brighten at Raymond's question. He answered, and Raymond fought down his fear and understood him to say, "Not my idea. The Harmers wanted to take you."

"Who are the Harmers?" he asked.

The Weeun pointed up at the crooky-staff, which Raymond still held above his head.

Raymond slowly lowered the crooky-staff but kept a tight hold on it, ready to use it at the first sign of trickery.

The Weeun nodded as the tip of the crooky-staff touched the ground and said, "The Harmers belong to our king. They keep him safe and carry out his orders."

Bort had described the evil looking Weeuns who marched in front of and behind the fat Weeun king. They must have been the Harmers.

"Are you a Harmer?"

The Weeun made a low sound like rocks falling onto a cobbie. Raymond gasped at the ugliness of it.

"Not me," the Weeun said and made the sound again.

It was a laugh. The Weeun was laughing at Raymond.

"Who are you, then, and what do you want?" he demanded angrily.

The Weeun looked nervously at the sleeping Bulkings by the fire.

"I am called Miffit," the Weeun said. "I am alone. They let me do what I please. I come and go as I like. Sometimes I follow the Harmers to see what terror they're doing for the king. Sometimes I sit and think and tell stories. No one minds me."

A Weeun as crazy as Wicker Bugle.

"How do you know the Bulking language? Do you speak it in your land?"

Miffit, the Weeun, shook his head. "Only a few know your language. The oldest of the olders wrote it down." The Weeun stood straighter. "I taught myself. No one bothered about my taking the old books. The language is useless to us."

Raymond concentrated on each word the Weeun said, trying not to feel the fear the sounds made inside him.

"How did you get here?" he asked.

"Under the ground. They've been digging and digging since before my own father was a baby. Now they have dug through, and there will be a great sadness."

"A sadness for who?"

The Weeun called Miffit clasped his hands together in front of his flat stomach.

"A sadness for everyone. For you. For us."

"You are not keeping with your king by telling me this," Raymond said. "How can I believe you? Why are you warning me against your own people?"

Miffit's eyes stared into Raymond's. He never seemed to blink. Raymond had to keep looking away to break the piercing contact, the feeling that he had no will.

"I do not care for the cruelty and death. After I entered your land and saw your ways, I had need to warn you. The Harmers will destroy you. There is more, more that I don't know. But I feel it will be a sadness for us, also."

"The Bulkings will be destroyed? Why does the king want to destroy us?"

Miffit shook his tiny head and pinched his thin arm.

"See how thin? Everyone is thin. There is not enough food to feed us. There are too many of us. Our families are

148

big, not little like yours. Long ago, a great wave came from the seas and destroyed the old lands. We had to move higher, close to the wall that separates our two lands.

"We were not wise with this weaker ground. The great wave was too sudden for us to take the good plants that grew in the old lands."

Miffit made his growling laugh. "When *my* great-greats ran from the great wave, they took their books first, and that was all they had time for. The tales say the giants know how to grow bigger plants, that the fruit and vegetables are stronger and sweeter in the land of the giants."

The Weeun spread his arms. "And I have been here and seen that it is true. There is plenty here. The king says that when the giants are gone, there will be more than plenty for all of us."

"We are not giants," Raymond told Miffit. "You are Weeuns. Tiny, tiny folk."

"We are not tiny. You are giants. The king does not want any giants left, even for slaves. He is afraid the Terror will happen again if there are any giants left, like in the tales."

The Terror must be the Finders' secret. Perhaps Raymond could discover it himself.

"What was the Terror?" he asked.

"I don't know. It happened when the giants escaped behind the great stone wall, long before the old lands were destroyed by the great wave and we were forced to move so close to the wall. Even the king does not know, but it is shameful to us and is only called the 'Terror.' "

"When will the Harmers invade Waterpushin?"

"Soon. The capture of the giant caused too much excitement; the king needs all the Harmers to keep the people calm."

So Gillus's capture had given them more time.

"What does the king want to do with Gillus, the Bulking who was captured?"

Miffit looked down at the ground and said in a quieter voice, "To kill him when the crowds have seen their fill and taunted him and done a thousand cruelties to him."

The Weeun spat on the ground in disgust.

To kill. Raymond had never heard of one Bulking killing another Bulking. Bulkings died of old age or sickness, or sometimes in accidents, but they were never killed.

"We are going to rescue him."

After a long silence, Miffit said, "Then you will be killed, too. The Harmers are very powerful."

Raymond sat on the grass. He was no longer afraid the Weeun would trick him. Even sitting down, the standing Weeun barely came to Raymond's shoulder.

"Then we will have to die. We can't just let a Bulking be killed."

The Weeun stood silently, and then said in wonder, "You would do that?"

"What other way is there?"

Miffit sat down a length from Raymond, his brows together in a Weeun frown.

Raymond got up and put more wood on the fire. In the new, bright blaze, he could see the closed eyes of Bort and Merrily; the hunched, still figure of Wicker Bugle. All sleeping.

When Raymond was finished, Miffit was still sitting in the lengthening moon shadows, his head on his small hands. Wicker Bugle stirred and moaned once. She didn't awaken, but the sound of her movements caused the Weeun to stand up hastily.

"I must leave now. There is something I must do. Will

you meet me in there," he pointed to the tunnel, "when the sun touches the tops of the trees?"

Raymond looked suspiciously at the Weeun, remembering the last time they'd met in the tunnel.

"Is this a trick?"

Miffit shook his head.

"The word of a Weeun is often made in trickery, but mine is not. There will be no trick. The Harmers will stay with the king today, I'm sure."

Miffit touched his cap. "If there is danger, I will leave my cap by the entrance as a sign that you should not enter."

Nearly hidden by the shadows, Miffit turned back to Raymond and asked, "Will you be there?"

"When the sun touches the tops of the trees," Raymond assured him, "I will enter the tunnel."

Miffit was gone. The forest and meadow were as silent and shadowy as if he'd never been there.

The sky to the east was turning pale when Raymond returned to the fire to waken Wicker Bugle.

20 · Treachery

ICKER BUGLE jerked wide awake when Raymond touched her shoulder.

"What's wrong?"

Her eyes were red from not enough sleep, and even in the glow from the dying fire and the rosy morning dawn, her skin was grayish. The book was open on her lap, and before Raymond could answer, she was running her knobby fingers across the lines of fine writing, searching for her lost place.

Raymond hesitated, then decided not to tell her of Miffit, the Weeun, or the planned meeting in the tunnel.

"Nothing's wrong," he told her. "I thought you'd want to continue working on the last book. You were asleep."

Indignation crossed her wrinkled face. "I was only resting," she said and turned her attention to the book, dismissing Raymond.

Raymond leaned on the crooky-staff and tried to sort out his feelings. Should he tell Bort and Merrily about Miffit? What if the Weeun didn't meet him in the tunnel as he'd promised? No, he'd best wait until after the meeting to tell.

"Did you think of ways to rescue Gillus?" Merrily asked hesitantly while they ate.

Bort and Raymond didn't answer.

"Neither did I," Merrily said and sighed. She put her

half-eaten bread on her lap. "It seems so impossible. We're too big to go through the Weeuns' underground passage."

"We don't even know where it is," Raymond said.

"The only other way is through the hollow in the Gartergates," Merrily said.

"The entire Weeun village would see us coming through the hollow," Bort told them. "Even their buildings aren't as tall as we are. Besides, the Gartergates are smooth and sheer on the side of the Weeuns. There are no toe- or handholds for climbing there."

They finished eating in hopeless silence.

Time crawled by as the day grew brighter and clearer. Raymond walked nervously around the meadow, peering into the dark forest, glancing down the tunnel, unable to sit still. He was aware of Bort's and Merrily's puzzled glances, but he ignored them.

Merrily was reading a book of Wicker Bugles's. It was filled with pale, beautiful drawings of the flowers and plants of Waterpushin. Under each drawing was a description of the plant and what it could be used for. Sometimes there was a notation in another handwriting next to the neat printing.

"Good for aching heads," one read. "Don't use on burns," said another. Still another in intriguing, faded penmanship said, "For love."

Bort sat with his back against the Gartergates. He was continually putting the spyglass to his eye. Sometimes he tried to follow the flight of a winger, other times he sought out some tiny crawler.

The sun touched the tops of the trees, turning them golden green.

"I'm going into the tunnel," Raymond said quickly to Merrily and Bort. "Wait for me here."

"Why?"

"Raymond, it's too dangerous to go alone."

"I'll be back. Wait for me," he said, and strode across the meadow toward the dark opening, leaving Merrily and Bort staring after him. Wicker Bugle didn't look up from the book.

There was no dark cap on the floor of the tunnel. Either there was no danger or Miffit hadn't returned from wherever he'd gone.

Raymond didn't want to be in the tunnel. The shadows lay thick and close. He fought the need to turn around and return to the meadow's light. Slowly he stepped forward, the crooky-staff ready. His mouth was dry. His tongue felt thick.

There was no sign of the Weeun. He took another step and glanced over his shoulder, afraid he might be cut off from returning to the meadow.

There was nothing behind him.

When he turned around again, the Weeun was standing in front of him. Raymond jumped, unable to stop the instant prickle of dread at seeing the tiny figure.

"Heelo," Miffit said in his hard little voice.

"Hello."

"I didn't trick you."

The Weeun seemed to be sadly considering Raymond. His shoulders slumped, and he looked smaller, weaker than he had in the meadow. Raymond turned his eyes from the Weeun's face.

"My father's father, many times back," the Weeun said, "came from across the Bluey Seas, searching for a better land than the one he'd left. He led the ship of Weeuns to this land. Many of the things that happened here were not good, but there was never anything as evil as what the king is planning now.

"I have been listening and watching this past while. The air is filled with betrayal and evil and . . . death."

He looked away and said softly to himself, "I am ashamed."

Raymond waited, afraid to say anything. There was a sorrow he couldn't understand.

"We are hungry, all of us but the king and the Harmers' families. There is not enough food, not enough . . ."

Miffit closed his round mouth tightly and bit his lip. Then he said fiercely, "The king means to attack your land tonight. He will march with the Harmers—he at the rear, of course. But once the Harmers are through the underground passage and your folk are destroyed, he means to let only the families of the Harmers through. Then the underground passage will be destroyed. There is a weakness built into the passage. The king will make it fall into itself.

"Nothing will be shared, as the king promised us. I can go wherever I please, and I have heard the king himself tell his plan. He only promised everyone better lives so we would work harder on the underground passage. It was a terrible treachery."

"What can we do?" Raymond asked.

"I have talked to your friend, Gillus," Miffit said.

"He is not my friend," Raymond said without thinking.

The Weeun looked at Raymond sadly.

"No matter. We are very different. We Weeuns and you Bulkings. So very different we could never live in the same land without one of us being destroyed. But now we must work together to save ourselves and each other.

155

"I have learned this much: The king and the Harmers will begin their attack when the moon rises tonight. Everyone will be at the underground passage, sending them off with cheers." Miffit spat. "At that time, I will unlock the cage of Gillus. It will be up to you to help him back into your land. He says he will return the same way he left."

"The door in the hollow," Raymond said. "What about the guards?"

"They will be with the king. There is no need to guard a land that is being betrayed." Miffit paused over the word, "betrayed," and then he said, "I know what I will do when the king and the Harmers have gone through the underground passage. In return, there is a promise I must ask of you."

Miffit was nearly finished telling Raymond what he wanted him to do when Merrily ran into the tunnel. She stopped with a shriek at the sight of Raymond talking to the Weeun.

"Don't forget," Miffit said and darted into the gloomy forest.

"A Weeun! You were talking to a Weeun!" Merrily said, her eyes wide and staring at the spot where Miffit had disappeared. She gave a start.

"Quick! Wicker Bugle has learned the secret language! You must come at once!"

The fatigue was gone from Wicker Bugle's face. She was reading slowly to Bort, who sat in front of her on the grass, leaning forward and listening attentively.

". . . the rocks are heavier and slower doing, no, going, than we thought. But Sullivan . . ." Wicker Bugle looked up at Merrily and said, "That must be your great-great, Sullivan Cumbers, Merrily."

She continued reading, "Sullivan says it must be done

156

this way. I am not the master stone layer that he is, although I am talented. All is in readiness: the stones set to be laid up, the secret door set into the hollow. That clever door is of my own design and manufacture. It is impossible to see it from either side.

"The crops from the new seeds are more bountiful than we'd hoped. There has been some quarreling today. Wilder Fibbey pretended to see a Weeun just to excite the men, who were resting after a particularly heavy stone. If it weren't for his great strength, I might wish he weren't with us."

Wicker Bugle stopped. "That's as far as I've gone. It's slow going, but now I can read it. I will be finished by afternoon."

"Raymond was in the tunnel talking to a Weeun!" Merrily blurted. "I saw him."

"Is this for true, Raymond?" Wicker Bugle asked.

"For true," Raymond replied. "The Weeun's name is Miffit."

Raymond told them of Miffit and the Weeun king's plan to destroy both his own folk and the Bulkings while he and the Harmers lived in plenty in Waterpushin.

"Never!" Wicker Bugle shouted and jumped up, her clenched fists in the air. The last book fell unheeded to the ground. Merrily leaped forward and picked it up, brushing off bits of grass with her hands.

"Now," Bort said. "Now is the time for us to tell the Majester."

"We'll make them believe us," added Raymond. "They have to."

"Go. Go now," Wicker Bugle said. "I will stay here until I have finished reading. We must know all the secrets of the Finders."

Merrily picked up the leather bag that the great Glom Gloom had made.

"We will need to show the Majester, to have proof," she said as she slung it over her shoulder.

"I still have the sharp stick," Raymond said.

"And the spyglass," Bort added.

"Go past my house to Gos," Wicker Bugle told them. "Gos will believe you and help you convince the others. It may not be safe to talk to the Majester first."

Wicker Bugle ran to her bag of belongings and took out a loose piece of paper.

"Put this in the bag," she said to Merrily. "It's the list of Bulkings who helped the Finders. It may help you convince the Majester."

Merrily opened the drawstrings enough to slide in the page, and they set out through the dark tunnel, back to Waterpushin.

21 · Telling the Majester

*T*HE SUN was marking midday when they passed Wicker Bugle's little house. The door was open and more of Wicker Bugle's belongings were strewn about.

"She was right," Merrily said. "They must have come here looking for her."

"And us," Raymond added.

Merrily shuddered.

There was no smoke coming from Gos's houseboat. Gos was sitting on a bench on the deck smoking a pipe of bacco and staring into the water.

The crooky-staff made soft "thwunk" sounds on the ground as Raymond walked. Gos took the pipe from his mouth and looked up.

When he saw them, Gos stood up and hurried down the narrow dock toward them. The rickety dock swung and creaked as he ran across it to meet them.

"Where's Gillus?" he asked. "What has happened?"

"The Weeuns have captured him," Raymond told him.

Gos staggered and gripped Raymond's arm.

"Is he . . .? Did they . . .?"

Merrily pushed past Raymond and touched Gos's shoulder.

"He's all right," she said gently. "Bort has seen him. But

159

we need your help to rescue him. We need the help of all the Bulkings."

"And Wicker Bugle? Do they have her, too?"

"She's at the Gartergates, reading the last book of Royal Bugle."

"So there really was a last book."

They quickly told Gos what they had discovered, about the Gartergates and the coming attack of the Weeuns.

"I have Glom Gloom's crooky-staff," Raymond said, holding out the staff.

Gos touched it reverently. He frowned at the bent top.

"It's a crutch," Raymond explained. "Glom Gloom had a lame leg."

"She said so," Gos said, "but I didn't want to believe that—not the great Finder."

Bort was on the deck of Gos's houseboat, searching through a pile of metals that Gos kept for mending and making new shapes. He pulled out a few long, thin pieces and set them aside.

"We may be able to use these," he said. "I saw the Weeuns carrying similar pieces . . . only much sharper."

Raymond took a piece of metal and held it in a way he imagined he might carry it into battle. Striking so, and just so . . .

"Careful," said Gos and took the metal from him. "First we must convince the Bulkings to do battle. It's not the Bulking way."

"Nor is it the Bulking way to let a fellow Bulking be killed at the hands of the Weeuns without trying to rescue him," said Raymond.

Gos nodded. "Well said, Raymond Fibbey. You carry your mouseling tail much higher now than you once did."

"We must hurry and tell the Majester about the Weeuns," Raymond told him.

"First," Gos said, "you must go to your own houses and explain to your parents what has happened. There has been much worry."

His parents. Raymond hadn't thought of his parents. He looked at Bort and Merrily and saw they were thinking the same thing. They had forgotten their parents in the danger of their adventure.

"I'll go to the Fish Barrelers," Gos told them. "They are all brave, good friends. We can meet in the square."

Loper Fibbey was in the garden digging when Raymond entered the gate. Warm Days never changed his habits, any more than holidays did. When he saw Raymond, he stopped digging and leaned against his shovel.

Raymond stood in front of him, his heart pounding.

After a long silence while Loper Fibbey stared thoughtfully at his son, he pointed to the crooky-staff and asked, "What's that you have there, Raymond?"

"It's the crooky-staff of Glom Gloom."

His father's expression didn't change.

"And what might you be doing with it?"

Raymond answered in a rush, trying to tell all at once.

"Our great-great, Wilder Fibbey, was with the Finders. He helped save the Bulkings from the Weeuns. And now the Weeuns have captured Gillus and are attacking Waterpushin tonight. We must save Waterpushin."

Loper Fibbey continued to look at his son. Raymond waited, unsure, as always, what his father might do or say.

"Your mother has been crying for two days," he finally said. "The Majester and the Search and Find team have been saying many things about you—and your friends. Are they for true?"

"Some of them," Raymond answered. "Because they had to be done. The Weeuns have come under the Garter-gates."

Loper Fibbey laid his shovel on the ground.

"What needs be done . . ." he said. "Let's go to your mother."

Dida Fibbey was sitting at the kitchen table, her hands folded in front of her. Tears shone on her cheeks.

When she saw Raymond, she stood up and put her arms around him, crying and laughing at the same time.

"Oh, Raymond. I thought . . . We thought, . . ."

Raymond hugged her briefly and stepped away.

"There are things I have to do before we leave."

"Leave?" Dida asked, blotting her wet eyes with her sleeve. "Where are we going? What has happened? The Majester said . . ."

Loper put his hand on his wife's arm and nodded to Raymond.

"This is the biggest trouble ever, Raymond. If . . ."

He didn't need to finish. Raymond understood what he was trying to tell him.

"I have seen the Weeuns myself," he said.

Loper nodded.

"You have changed," he said. "Do what you need. I will explain to your mother, and we will wait here for you."

Raymond gave the crooky-staff to his father, who took it with the same wondering glance at the bent top that Raymond had once given it.

"He was lame," Raymond said.

In his room, Raymond emptied his cloth bag on his bed. He took the silver Tiny of the Gartergates and slipped it into his pocket.

The map was still under his bed, rolled up and tied as he'd left it. He pulled it out and took it to the kitchen.

His father was sharpening a knife, and his mother was wrapping paturnie cakes in brown paper. Raymond set the map on the table.

"It's the map that was stolen from Gimly School," he said.

His mother gasped.

"I'll return it to the Majester. Now I must quickly do something I promised."

When Raymond returned, his cloth bag bulged on his shoulder. His mother and father were waiting in the coolish kitchen. Two cloth bags were leaning against the door. One large, one small, both bulging. Dida was wearing her red and yellow holiday cloak, and Loper had tied a red and yellow band of cloth around his arm.

His father held out a hat to him. It was old and gray and nearly shapeless. One brim was turned up, held by a large pin with a flat end painted red and yellow.

"It was my father's," Loper Fibbey told Raymond, "and his father's. I don't know who it first belonged to, but I have never worn it. Now you should wear it."

Raymond held the hat in his hands. It was soft and well-used. There was a dark ring of sweat in its inside. When he put the hat on, it fit perfectly to his head. Loper Fibbey nodded and gave the crooky-staff back to him.

The Fibbeys looked neither right nor left, as they walked together to the square, paying no attention to the whispers and questioning stares of the Bulkings.

Everyone knew Raymond was in trouble. Was the whole family in trouble? The Bulkings trickled into the cobbies behind the Fibbey family.

As they neared the square, Raymond saw another procession coming from the other side of the village. It was Bort and his family, followed by more Bulkings. And from the direction of the Waterpush, came the Fish Barrelers, singing a rollicking song and headed up by Gos, who was carrying a strip of metal like a music conductor.

In the square, in front of the Majester's old house, stood the Majester watching the three processions descend upon him. The five members of his council stood disapprovingly behind him. Opposite the Majester, Merrily Cumbers stood, with her mother and father standing sternly behind her. Merrily's face was red and angry. Her lips were held so tightly they barely showed.

"And we're the best." The Fish Barrelers ended their song and stood silently behind Gos, holding all different-sized strips of metal: barrel wrappers, wagon supports.

The watching Bulkings pointed to the strips of metal, murmuring and frowning over the strange sight.

"What is happening here?" the Majester bellowed, his voice carrying across the square and echoing over their heads.

Raymond swallowed and tried to work spit around his dry mouth. Gripping the crooky-staff so hard his palm hurt, he stepped forward, holding the map in front of him.

"I took the map," he said in a dry whisper, and gave it to the Majester.

The Bulkings in the square murmured, asking each other what Raymond had said.

"I took the map," Raymond repeated, louder, more firmly.

"Aaaah," a sigh went through the crowd and someone said loudly, "We might have known . . . Raymond Fibbey."

The Majester opened the rolled map, nodding in satisfaction that it was undamaged. He gave it to the leading member of his council.

"Why did you take the map, Raymond?" Majester Trader asked, not unkindly.

"I wanted to find the Gartergates, to see if they were for true."

"The Gartergates are part of the great story—" the Majester began, but Merrily jumped forward.

"They're for true," she said loudly, "and the Weeuns have come through them."

Merrily's father made a step forward, but the Majester motioned him back.

"We've seen the Weeuns," Bort said, stepping up to join Raymond and Merrily.

The crowd of Bulkings began to whisper excitedly.

The leading council member raised his arms. "Silence!" he shouted, and the crowd reluctantly turned from each other.

"You children . . ." the Majester said, shaking his head.

"I believe them," Loper Fibbey said and put his hand on Raymond's shoulder.

"And I," added Bort's father. "Show the Majester the spyglass."

Bort took the spyglass from his tunic. "It belonged to my great-great, Bartholomew Dare Gard. You can see his name written on the side of it. We found it at the Gartergates."

The Majester held the spyglass up to the afternoon sun and read the fine writing along its side.

"And the leather bag," Merrily said, taking it from her shoulder and holding it out to the Majester.

"What was in the bag?" he asked.

"The spyglass and the book written by Royal Bugle."

"Royal Bugle?" The Majester frowned. "Where is the book?"

Merrily hesitated. "Wicker Bugle is reading it to discover how the Finders defeated the Weeuns."

"Wicker Bugle!" Merrily's mother cried. "She's led these children into nonsense!"

"Wicker Bugle . . ."

"That crazy old haggie."

"Wicker Bugle tricked them!"

"Silence!" the council member shouted again and the crowd slowly quieted.

"I have Glom Gloom's crooky-staff," Raymond told the Majester.

The Majester examined the crooky-staff, feeling the smooth, hard wood. "This can't be Glom Gloom's crooky-staff. It's a crutch."

"Glom Gloom's crooky-staff," someone said scornfully, and the crowd laughed.

Gos held up his arms.

"We Bulkings have been foolish," he said. "The Finders were Bulkings, like us. Glom Gloom's crooky-staff looks like a crutch because it *is* a crutch. Glom Gloom was lame. But that doesn't make him any less a hero. The Finders didn't ask to be turned into magic tales."

Gos took a deep breath that could be heard in the hushed square.

"The Weeuns have Gillus. He is my charge, as close to me as any son. I may not be a brave Bulking, but I refuse to let the Weeuns keep him. *I* will at least try to rescue him."

Merrily's parents stood grimly.

166

"I cannot believe it," Merrily's father said.

"Nor I."

". . . not the Bulking way."

"Raymond," Bort said, nudging him with his elbow, "What about the list of names?"

"Look in the leather bag, Majester Trader," Raymond said. "There is a list of Bulkings who helped the Finders build the Gartergates and rescue the Bulkings from the Weeuns."

The Majester pulled out the heavy piece of paper. His lips moved as he read the names. "Scovie Trader?" he said aloud.

"Your great-great," said Raymond.

"My great-great," the Majester repeated.

"I have a list of names here," the Majester said, waving the paper above his head. "Raymond Fibbey says it is a list of Bulkings who helped the Finders."

Someone snorted in disbelief. Both the Majester and Loper Fibbey glared in the direction of the noise.

The Majester read the names, pausing after each one. There were gasps from the crowd as the names were recognized.

As he said, "Sullivan Cumbers," Merrily's parents turned to each other.

"I remember old stories," Merrily's father said uncertainly, "but I never believed . . ."

Loper Fibbey said to Merrily's father, "Aye, I thought the stories were just an older's ramblings."

"Can it be for true, then?"

"I believe it," said Loper.

Majester Trader finished the list with, "And to the impatient, distruthful Wilder Fibbey, to whom we perhaps all owe our lives."

Loper Fibbey coughed in a mixture of embarrassment and pride.

The Majester touched the leather bag, feeling its texture with his fingers.

"This bag," he said. "I know this bag. There is another like it." He scratched his ear. "When we moved to the new house, there was a stack of old, useless things we left behind in the old house. Among these was a bag very much like this." He turned to one of the council members. "Do you remember it?" he asked.

The council member shrugged. "There were many useless things in that pile."

"Go find it," the Majester ordered.

There was a disturbance at the edge of the crowd.

"Let me through! Let me through," an angry voice demanded.

As her voice was recognized, her name went through the crowd like a wind.

"Wicker Bugle. Wicker Bugle."

She came out of the crowd and strode toward the Majester, the last book clasped in her arms. She was smiling, more brilliantly than Raymond had ever seen her smile.

"I have read it!" she said. "I have read the last book, and it's so simple."

She threw back her head and laughed deeply, wildly. The Bulkings in the crowd watched uncertainly. Crazy old haggie.

"So simple," Wicker Bugle repeated. She poked Raymond. "Your great-great, Wilder Fibbey, was very much like you," she said and laughed again.

The Majester's wife was standing beside the Majester, talking earnestly and quietly to him, her face pale.

The Majester leaned toward Raymond, Bort and Merrily, including Wicker Bugle in his glance.

"You say you have seen the Weeuns," he said softly. "Tell me what they look like."

They told him of the tiny, round-eyed Weeuns. The Majester's face grew whiter with each word.

The Majester's wife leaned closer. "And do they wear little caps on their heads?" she asked.

"Aye," Bort told her, "to keep the hair out of their eyes."

The Majester's wife put her hand to her mouth and fainted. The crowd gasped as she fell. The Majester caught her, saying, "My dear, my dear."

Dida and Bort's mother helped the Majester's wife, fanning her face and patting her wrists.

"Our daughter," the Majester said, "our Trillia, told us of such a creature beside her bed in the new house." He put a hand to his forehead. "We thought she was dreaming. In my own house . . . In my own house."

The Majester pulled himself tall and turned to the waiting crowd.

"The Weeuns have invaded Waterpushin," he said gravely, and then commanded, "Go to your homes and make ready, then return here."

The Bulkings left the square, some walking in a daze, others running in fright, their voices rising in fear and confusion.

"What are we to do?" the Majester asked.

"I have learned the secret," Wicker Bugle reminded him. "We will defeat the Weeuns. When the Bulkings return, I will tell them the secret, and they will not be so frightened."

The council member returned from the old house. He was dusty but he held a leather bag in his arms.

The Majester took it and opened the draw strings, coughing at the dust. From inside, he pulled out a leather-covered book. He opened the cover and read aloud, "For the Bulkings of Waterpushin. To always be kept safe."

"It is the story of the escape from the Weeuns!" Wicker Bugle said excitedly. "The book written in the Bulking language by my great-great. He said he had written a book for the Bulkings to always keep, to remember."

"It was put aside," the Majester said.

"Forgotten," Merrily added.

"Like old trash," added Loper Fibbey.

Wicker Bugle sat on the cobbie stones in the square. "Now you can read along with me," she said.

They sat around her, the Majester holding the precious book in the Bulking language. Wicker Bugle opened Royal Bugle's last book on her lap and began to read the long lost words.

22 · The Rescue

HILE they waited for the square to fill with Bulkings, Raymond, Bort and Merrily told the Majester how they had come to discover the Gartergates. Wicker Bugle told all she'd learned from her great-greats: of the strange hypnotic powers of the Weeuns, of the determination and bravery of the Finders.

The parents listened, occasionally turning to each other and glancing at their children in wonder.

The Bulkings returning to the square wore bright red and yellow holiday colors. Some carried cloth bags, some had weapons of sticks or strips of metal.

"We should divide into two groups," Raymond said to the Majester, "one group to go to the Gartergates, one to stay and defend the village . . . if need be."

"Aye," Wicker Bugle agreed. "That is the best plan."

"You'd best stay here in the village," Raymond heard his father say to his mother.

"No," Dida said firmly. "I'll not stay behind. I'm going with you and Raymond."

Loper Fibbey opened his mouth to answer, but Dida folded her arms and said, "That's final. I'm coming with you."

Raymond and Bort would go to the Gartergates; Merrily and her family would stay with the village defenders. Wicker Bugle refused to be part of either group.

"I want to see as much as I can and be as many places as possible," she said. "Then I will write a new book about Waterpushin and the Weeuns."

"In a secret language?" Raymond asked.

"No," she said. "This book will only be in the language of the Bulkings, and what is for true will be for true, not turned into fanciful stories to be laughed out of memory by forgetful Bulkings."

The Majester stepped up on the speech block and spoke to the hushed crowd.

"We are Bulkings," he said, "proud Bulkings. We have been foolish, too secure. We were too eager to put away the stories of our olders."

Raymond fidgeted, wanting to be on the way. The time for speeches had long since run out. His father put a steadying hand on his shoulder, and Raymond could see his own impatience mirrored on his father's controlled face.

"But now we have come together in a better understanding of our past . . . ."

Other Bulkings in the crowd began to fidget and exchange glances with one another.

"Let no Bulking forget his or her honor tonight, the honor given back to us by three young Bulkings in our midst."

"Don't forget Wicker Bugle!"

Raymond recognized Merrily's voice.

The Majester coughed slightly and said, "Yes, and Wicker Bugle."

Wicker Bugle closed her eyes and inclined her head graciously at the recognition.

"Let us go," the Majester finished. "Good Gloom to you."

"Good Gloom! Good Gloom!" the crowd returned.

The village defenders walked with the procession going to the Gartergates as far as the Majester's new house on Majester's Hill.

Wicker Bugle bustled back and forth between the Bulkings.

"Don't be forgetting how the Finders conquered the Weeuns," she said. "Don't be forgetting the secret."

And always, the refrain, "Good Gloom, Good Gloom to you," could be heard.

The village defenders watched soberly as the forces moved off Majester's Hill toward the Gartergates.

"It may be a long night," Bort said to Raymond.

"Aye."

"Raymond! Bort!"

It was Merrily, running to catch up with them. They stepped out of the procession and waited for her. She held out a hand to each of them and squeezed their hands.

"When you return . . ." she said and turned and ran back toward Majester Trader's house.

In the first meadow Raymond told them what Miffit the Weeun had said, "The Weeuns will enter Waterpushin through their underground passage between here and the Gartergates," he waved toward the thick forest.

"We'd best divide the force between here and the Gartergates," Gos said.

Bort pointed up to a protruding rock in the sharp cliff that ran along the edge of the meadow.

"If I could get up there, I might be able to see the Weeuns approaching. I would be above the trees and with the spy glass . . ."

"Zeed, here," one of the Fish Barrelers said, pointing to the Fish Barreler beside him, "can stand on my shoulders. We've done it many a time. If Bort were lifted to his shoulders, he could mayhap reach the stone."

In no time Zeed was balancing on his friend's shoulders. Bort was easily handed up to Zeed. From there Zeed lifted Bort until he could scramble onto the protruding rock.

"I can see the Gartergates," he called down, pointing toward the smooth gray Gartergates.

Although nothing but the forest could be seen from the meadow, the Bulkings looked in the direction Bort was pointing. The Gartergates!

"It's time to go to the Gartergates and make ready," Wicker Bugle said, stepping into the tunnel.

"Good Gloom," Raymond said behind him as he entered the tunnel, looking up one last time at the small, skinny figure of Bort perched on the side of the cliff.

They hurried through the tunnel, the dark secretive tunnel, like a long trap.

At the sight of the Gartergates, Loper Fibbey breathed a deep sigh.

"I never thought . . ." he said.

The others stared in reverence. The smooth gray stones of the Gartergates glowed softly as they were touched by the last rays of the sun.

Raymond pointed to the dark hole in the Gartergates. "There's the hollow Gillus will be coming through. I must go up and wait for him."

In the spot where Bort and Merrily and Raymond had camped the night before, furthest from the tunnel and the thick forest, Loper Fibbey arranged the cloth bags so that they formed a low, semi-circular wall.

"Stay here until I come for you," he said to Dida, "no matter what happens."

Loper touched Dida's cheek gently and returned to Raymond. Dida stared after him, her hand to her cheek.

"Should a Bulking child be the one to attempt the rescue of Gillus?" one of the Fish Barrelers asked.

Raymond felt a quick fear. What if they wouldn't allow him? What would happen if he didn't keep his promise to the red-haired Weeun?

"Raymond has proven himself to be more than a mere Bulking child," Raymond's father said with such sternness and finality that the matter was settled.

Raymond adjusted his bulky cloth bag over his shoulder and then slipped the coil of rope he'd brought over his other shoulder.

"It's a heavy load," Loper said.

"Not too."

The sun no longer shone on the Gartergates. In the dusky light, the toe and hand holds were impossible to see. Raymond had to feel along the smooth rock for each one. The cloth bag and rope chafed against his shoulders, and his hands were skinned raw. He breathed slowly, trying to relax. Finally his hand touched the opening of the hollow. Almost there.

Raymond pulled himself inside the hollow on his stomach, gratefully feeling the cool, dampish floor beneath him. There was room to sit up if he bent his head forward and curved his back. The hollow was no wider than the distance between his elbows if he tried to stretch his arms.

Raymond dropped one end of the rope down to his father until there was just enough to reach the ground. By the fading light from the hollow's opening, Raymond tied large knots in the other end of the rope: one at the very end, another a length further, and another still further up.

"When you feel a pull on the rope, pull it as fast and as hard as you're able," Raymond called down in a low voice.

"Aye," several voices softly answered.

The door opened smoothly. The clamoring of Weeun voices blasted into the hollow. Raymond felt the horrible fear, the need to run, to get away. The voices seemed to be cheering, and there was strange music and the singing of a low, grating song.

A parade of lights was ascending the hill from the Weeun village. Bobbing, twinkling, coming together, then apart. Every Weeun in the land must be coming up the hill.

As the parade approached, Raymond could see that in the midst of the bobbing, erratic lights, there was another procession. This one was an orderly straight line of double lights, led by the makers of the strange music.

The Harmers.

Just behind the music-makers marched a single figure. From its roundness, Raymond knew it must be the king.

The sight of hundreds of Weeuns and the sounds of their voices nearly paralyzed him. He watched with his mouth open, the fear so strong he could hardly breathe.

Then he remembered Gillus. He took the bits of cotton Wicker Bugle had given him and pushed them into his ears. The sound of the Weeuns receded, and he could think more clearly.

Where *was* Gillus? Raymond searched the hill for Gillus's figure. What if Miffit hadn't been able to unlock the cage? Even in the darkness Gillus should be easy to see.

If Gillus weren't there soon, the Weeuns would be close to the Gartergates, and it would be too late.

Just then, Raymond spotted Gillus coming from the village. The dark figure was bending close to the ground, hunched but moving rapidly up the opposite side of the hill from the Weeuns. Raymond winced at Gillus's bulk. Giants, Miffit had called the Bulkings. The Weeuns only needed to turn and look. There was no way to hide a Bulking among Weeuns.

Gillus was nearly there. Raymond could see that something was wrong with Gillus's shoulder. His arm hung awkwardly.

Raymond leaned out the door and dropped the rope. It nearly touched the ground.

The Weeuns had reached the entrance of the underground passage. Raymond could see it clearly in the many tiny lights. The music-makers were standing in front of the entrance playing a song. Through the bits of cotton, it sounded to Raymond like water crashing on rocks. The Weeuns all stood listening.

Gillus stood and ran to the Gartergates. The Weeuns broke into an angry buzz, and the musicians stopped playing in a strangle of sounds. One of the bits of cotton fell from Raymond's ears, but he didn't dare let go of the rope and replace it.

"Gillus! Take the rope!"

Gillus looked up at Raymond, confused, touching his useless arm.

The lights of the Weeuns were heading their way, coming in a haphazard rush. The angry buzz grew to a roar that filled Raymond with desperation.

"Take the rope! Stand on the knot. Hold on with one arm! Just take the rope, and we'll do the rest. Do you want them to catch you again?"

Gillus took the rope with his good hand. Then he

hesitated, his eyes suddenly distant as if he were about to turn and go toward the approaching Weeuns.

The sound of the Weeuns was terrifying. Raymond wanted to pull back inside the hollow and shut the door. He wanted to leave Gillus. The Weeuns were slowing to fit tiny sharp sticks into bows. Gillus winced as one struck his leg.

"Gillus!" Raymond screamed. "Take the rope or I'm leaving you to the Weeuns!"

Gillus looked up at Raymond as if he were awakening from a daze. He stepped onto the knotted rope end and held the higher knot with his good hand.

Raymond jerked the rope and felt it being pulled from the other side of the Gartergates. Gillus rose above the Weeuns. He jounced against the side of the Gartergates, crying out once when his hurt shoulder took the brunt of the blow. For an instant, Raymond thought he was going to let go of the rope.

"Almost here, Gillus . . . almost here . . . just hang on a little longer," he repeated as the top of Gillus's head came closer and closer to the hollow. The Weeuns were shooting their sharp sticks at Gillus in volleys. They stuck into his legs and body. He winced and moaned when one struck his cheek, bringing blood trickling down his jaw.

"I can't. I can't," he said and started to slump.

Raymond leaned forward as far as he dared. His fingers just touched Gillus's head. He twined his fingers among the thick strands of Gillus's hair and pulled as hard as he could.

The noise of the Weeuns grew louder when they saw Raymond helping Gillus. Raymond felt the sharp prick of one of their sticks in his hand, but he held on to Gillus's hair, pulling him into the hollow.

Then Raymond lay with Gillus half on top of him. He was glad Gillus was unconscious, because the pulling and turning of Gillus's body had forced the sharp sticks deeper into his flesh.

The angry Weeuns beneath them were shouting wildly, but they seemed to be moving away. Raymond removed the sharp stick from his hand, grimacing from the pain. The end of this stick was barbed, more painful than the sharp, smooth sticks shot at him in the tunnel. He pushed Gillus aside as best he could in the narrow hollow and looked out the door.

The angry Weeuns were heading for the entrance to the underground passage. There the king was motioning the Harmers into the entrance. He waved a long lance and shouted in his deep, ugly voice. The Weeuns from the village screamed and shouted in approval, waving their lights like weapons.

With a thud, Raymond pulled the door closed and fell back beside Gillus. The sounds of the Weeuns were gone as if they had been cut off.

"Raymond," Gillus whispered.

"Yes?"

"Did we make it?"

"I think so, but the Weeuns are on their way into Waterpushin."

Gillus swallowed and turned his head to spit.

"I hurt," he said.

"Raymond?" came a voice from outside the hollow.

It was Raymond's father, holding tightly to the side of the Gartergates just below the opening.

"Here," Raymond told him.

"Gillus?"

"Here, also, but hurt."

"And what of the Weeuns?"

"They're on their way through the underground passage. They saw Gillus escape, and they're frantic with anger."

"I have your mother's cloak around my shoulders. Wrap it around Gillus, if you can, and slide him down the cliff to us. Your mother is ready for him."

Raymond reached down and unclasped his mother's holiday cloak from his father's shoulders and pulled it into the hollow.

"That red-haired Weeun," Gillus said.

"What about him?" Raymond asked. He pulled a barbed stick from Gillus's arm, drawing it out as quickly as he could. Gillus gasped.

"He let me out. Said to tell you he was going to close off the underground passage in an hour's time after the Weeuns went through. He said that was the best he could do. The rest was up to us Bulkings."

"Did he say anything else?" Raymond asked.

"Not to forget your promise. To keep it after the underground passage was closed off."

Raymond wrapped the cloak around Gillus. Gillus slipped in and out of wakefulness, moaning softly in his pain.

"I'm going to slide you down the Gartergates, Gillus," Raymond told him. "It will probably hurt worse than anything so far, but it's the only way to get you down."

"I understand," Gillus said weakly.

Raymond's father and Gos and four Fish Barrelers were waiting below.

"I'm going to have to push him out head first," Raymond called down. "I can't turn him."

"We'll catch him," Gos said.

As Raymond moved Gillus, Gillus asked, "There never was any treasure, was there?"

"No."

Raymond gave Gillus a hard shove, and he slid down the Gartergates in a rush, head first. Raymond hoped he was unconscious again.

"We've got him," Gos called up to Raymond.

Raymond left his cloth bag in the hollow and climbed down the Gartergates.

23 · The Battle

THE MOON was rising above the Green Mountains, just touching the tops of the trees in greenish brightness. Bort sat high on the rock above the Bulkings, searching the dark forest with his spyglass.

Beneath him, his father and the other Bulkings restlessly waited.

"See anything yet?" someone would call up every little bit.

"Not yet. Still looking," Bort would call down each time.

He shivered in sudden cold once when he thought he heard a deep sound coming from the direction of the Gartergates, but when he looked through the spyglass he saw nothing.

A glimmer of light flashed in the trees deep in the forest.

"Wait! I see something."

The Bulkings jumped to their feet.

There it was again. A light low in the forest. He was sure of it. Then it was gone.

"I saw a light," he said without taking his eyes from the spot where it had briefly glowed. The moon was higher in the sky, and he saw movement in the forest. Bushes were moving as if being brushed against. There was a sound like low buzzing. Even as faint as the sound was, Bort recognized the Weeun sound. His hands shook. The Weeuns weren't being as careful as he'd expected. They didn't seem to care about creeping up on the Bulkings.

"I can see a line of movement coming this way."

Bort pointed in the direction, and the Bulkings turned to face that way.

"Wait! Now it seems to be going toward the Gartergates. No, it's a second line!"

"They're going to attack us both at once," Bort's father said. "We'd better warn the others."

"I'll go to the Gartergates," Bort called down.

"No, you stay there. We need your eyes."

Jerem, Bort's brother, stepped forward. "I'll go," he said. Bort's father hesitated, then said, "Hurry, then." Jerem looked up at Bort for the briefest moment. "Good Gloom," Bort said, and Jerem nodded.

✳ ✳ ✳

GILLUS was lying inside the low wall of cloth bags that Loper Fibbey had made. Dida Fibbey had already tied a splint around his arm and shoulder, and it stuck stiffly out by his side. Now she was pulling the sharp sticks from Gillus's body. She cleaned and bandaged each wound with supplies from the cloth bags.

"It'll be over soon . . . just a few more," she crooned to Gillus.

"Thank you," Gillus whispered again and again.

Bort's brother came rushing out of the tunnel, startling them so much that one of the Fish Barrelers nearly threw a wicked piece of metal at him.

"They're coming!" Jerem said breathlessly. "Two groups of them. One in this direction and one toward the meadow where the others are."

Jerem turned and ran back into the tunnel. Wicker Bugle rushed after him.

Wordlessly, the Fish Barrelers and Bulkings formed in front of Gillus and Dida. They stood silently, staring into the dark tangled forest.

Waiting. Raymond felt his heart pounding so loudly he expected the Bulking next to him to comment on it.

Would the secret work? It seemed so simple, foolish almost. He remembered their surprise when they had sat together in the square, the Majester holding the book in Bulking language and Wicker Bugle reading to them from Royal Bugle's book.

" 'And so,' " she had read excitedly, " 'Wilder Fibbey saved us all by losing his temper, that terrible temper, which has, until now, caused nothing but trouble.

" 'We were nearly to the Gartergates, nearly to safety. We had convinced the enslaved Bulkings to follow us to Waterpushin, a land of safety. We led them away by day-light while the Weeuns rested. The Weeuns had become too sure of their captives over the seasons to guard them any longer.

" 'It was not hard to convince the Bulkings to leave. So many had died by the Weeuns.

" 'We were almost to the Gartergates, when suddenly there were Weeuns on every side of us with their sharp weapons and that horrible grinding noise that touches some terrible fear in us. Those we were leading were too new to freedom, the fear of the Weeun power too fresh in their hearts. At the first sound of a child crying out, they were ready to surrender. We did not know what to do. We could barely move for the fear their voices and wicked visages struck in us. All was chaos and seemingly lost.

" 'But then, with a horrible roar, Wilder Fibbey lost his temper. His face was frightening to see. It turned red and purple, and his mouth opened wide and his forehead wrinkled. He put his fingers into his ears, closing out the sounds of the Weeun voices.

" ' "You'll not take them back, you ugly round-eyed Wigglers!" he shouted. Then he threw back his head and roared his terrible rage, a roar louder than I had ever heard. It was a roar of anger and frustration and what we were all feeling: hopelessness.

" 'The effect on the Weeuns was startling. Wilder Fibbey's roaring caused a horrible pain to the Weeuns. Several paused uncertainly, staring at Wilder Fibbey. A few faltered and dropped their weapons, doubling over and covering their ears as if they'd been struck.

" 'When Glom Gloom saw the effect of Wilder Fibbey's roaring, he hurried beside Wilder and began to imitate him. Loud shrieks and terrible faces coming from the quiet Glom Gloom!

" ' "Don't look into their faces! Don't look!" Glom Gloom shouted, covering his ears and balancing on his crutch.

" 'For some moments I stared in disbelief before I too ran forward and imitated Glom Gloom and Wilder Fibbey. I tore my nose cloth into tiny pieces and gave bits to Wilder and Glom Gloom. I have never known Bulkings to act in such a way, and the combination of our throat-scorching roars and our appearance touched the core of the Weeuns in the same way their voices and strange eyes and sharp weapons frighten us.

" 'Other Bulkings stuffed their ears and began shouting

and screeching and making horrid faces and marching toward the surrounding Weeuns.

" ' "Don't look into their eyes! Keep away from their eyes!" we warned each other. We were frightened, all of us, as we discussed later over warm grog for our sore throats.

" 'The Weeuns made strange whimpering noises in their throats. They turned from us and ran back toward their land, dropping their weapons along the way and bumping into each other in their fright.

" 'We then entered the land of Waterpushin and sealed off the Gartergates. We will live in gentleness again. It is shameful that we acted as we did, even though it saved our lives. We can live in our peaceful manner now, without fear. If only the Gartergates be kept strong, it need never happen again,' " Wicker Bugle had finished.

Now Raymond hoped it was still true, that the passing of many seasons hadn't changed the fear of the Weeuns.

"Raymond."

It was Teacher Joiner, holding a garden rake and still wearing the emblem of the Search and Find team.

"Many times, you have caused much trouble . . ."

Was Teacher Joiner going to lecture him *now?*

Teacher Joiner smiled. "But it is good you took the map. It—"

"Sssst." A Bulking to the side hissed in warning.

There was a rustling of bushes, and several tiny Weeuns bounded into the moonlit meadow. They carried raised weapons and were making low, growling sounds.

There were twenty, thirty, then maybe forty, scurrying to form a loose line against the trees, facing the Bulkings.

"Good Gloom," Teacher Joiner whispered and began stuffing torn bits of cloth into his ears.

186

Raymond felt a cold, cold fear and the compulsion to run in the opposite direction. He pushed the bits of cotton into his ears until all he heard was the pounding of his own heart.

Dark as the shadows, dark as the dense forest, with the glowing round eyes that never seemed to blink, the Weeuns were ready. Their pale round faces jerked from side to side, watching the Bulkings.

The Bulkings stood transfixed as the Weeuns spread further out into the meadow. The small bodies leaned forward as they ran. The wicked weapons were raised, catching the silvery glints of bright moonlight.

And still the Bulkings stood unmoving, hypnotized by the sight of the Weeuns preparing to do battle.

"Don't look at them! Don't look!" Dida Fibbey shouted with a terrified cry from behind them, and the Bulkings jumped at the sound of her voice, their trances broken.

Loper Fibbey made a great roaring sound that Raymond could feel through his plugged ears. Raymond held the crooky-staff of Glom Gloom high in the air and started to roar like his father, but his voice caught and the roar came out like a child's screech. His father turned to him and nodded encouragement.

The Weeuns came to an immediate stop, their weapons still raised but their voices silenced. Other Bulkings followed Raymond and Loper Fibbey's lead: raising their arms, shouting and making horrible faces.

A few of the Weeuns took cautious backward steps, but a Weeun with a wicked barbed weapon gave a throaty order, and the Weeuns began marching forward.

Raymond roared again past the dryness in his throat and took another step forward. He felt the urge to look into the round, round eyes and quickly glanced about him, away from the Weeuns. He saw Teacher Joiner standing silent behind him, his arms loose at his side and his eyes staring.

Again the Weeuns halted, and a few ran back into the forest despite the shouted orders from their leader.

It was true. The fear of the Bulkings was great, but the fear of the Weeuns was greater. The Bulkings advanced on the Weeuns, one step at a time, roaring and grimacing and waving their arms, acting as they never had before. The Weeuns turned and ran, some holding their heads in pain, plunging back into the forest one after another.

Weapons that had glowed so ferociously in the moonlight now shone palely in the grass of the meadow.

Raymond bellowed, feeling a strange gladness. The Weeuns were running. They were afraid.

"We have to follow them, to chase them back into the underground passage!" Raymond shouted.

Whether they had heard him through their stuffed ears or not, the Fish Barrelers leaped forward and began hacking at the thick brush with their short knives and thin strips of metal.

The way through the dense forest seemed impossibly slow. The Bulkings hacked and slashed at the thick growth, all the time making the terrible sounds. Raymond beat at the brush with Glom Gloom's crooky-staff, trying to widen the way, to hurry the Weeuns toward the underground passage. There was a path, a small path hacked out by the Weeuns, which they followed. It was like following the trail of a rabbit. Too tiny to walk on.

The Bulkings were scratched and sweat-covered and their clothes were torn when they finally came to a widening in the trail. There the trail opened into a small clearing. And in the middle of the clearing was a mound of dirt and a smallish hole in the ground.

The other end of the underground passage.

A Weeun poked his cap-covered head out of the underground passage, and one of the Fish Barrelers gave a loud roar. The Weeun disappeared back inside the hole.

Raymond removed one piece of cloth from his ears and motioned to the others to do the same.

"We must hide here in the trees and wait to be sure all the Weeuns go inside the underground passage," Raymond said.

"Then we should close off the opening," Gos said.

"I think something else may happen," Raymond replied. Gos looked at him questioningly but said nothing.

In a rustle and a rush, troops of Weeuns ran into the clearing from the opposite direction and scurried into the underground passage, not even glancing toward the trees where Raymond and the others were hiding.

At the end of the troop, the fat king puffed and shouted angrily at his men. His cap was askew and his hair pushed out in every direction. The king's men, the Harmers, paid no attention to him. They jumped into the underground passage, leaving the king to save himself. The king was the final Weeun into the hole.

Every little while one or more of the Weeuns would cautiously try to leave the underground passage, but the Bulkings jumped into the clearing, roaring and shouting until the Weeuns hastily returned to the dark hole in the ground. Once a volley of sharp sticks came from the underground passage, but they fell harmlessly to the ground in the clearing

Eventually, a tattered Wicker Bugle and Bort and more Bulkings entered the moonlit clearing. Raymond motioned for them to stay back in the thick forest.

Suddenly there was a rumbling sound. At first it seemed a far away echo. The Bulkings looked around them in puzzlement. Then it seemed to be coming from the underground passage. It grew louder and louder.

"What . . ." began Gos.

The rumbling turned into crashing. Grinding rock falling on rock. Dust filled the clearing and the noses and eyes of the waiting Bulkings. Raymond covered his eyes with his hands.

The crashing died to a low rumbling. It fell further and further away until there was only fine dust in the air and the silence of the forest.

Raymond uncovered his eyes. The opening was filled with dirt and rocks.

The Bulkings stood for a while in front of the closed-off underground passage, staring silently at the dirt and rocks that filled the hole. They didn't speak, each of them thinking about what had happened inside the underground passage. There had been terrible death. They all knew that. They had never known so much death.

Death. Killing. It was not the Bulking way.

Yet if the Weeuns hadn't died, the Bulkings would have died. Over and over, inside each Bulking's mind, was the refrain, "If they hadn't died, we would have died."

Even so . . .

* * *

WHEN they entered the meadow by the Gartergates, Dida Fibbey was standing in the middle, her hands over her mouth as she watched her fellow Bulkings straggle into the bright clearing. When she saw Loper and Raymond, she gave a little gasp and ran to them, putting an arm around each.

Loper Fibbey patted her back and said gruffly, "You didn't think we'd be harmed, did you?"

The Bulkings silently applied ointments and bandages to their wounds. They made a stretcher to carry Gillus and repacked their cloth bags.

Raymond readied himself to climb to the hollow in the Gartergates. Only his father noted his preparations.

"I have a promise to keep," Raymond told him.

His father nodded and stood by to watch him wearily climb the Gartergates.

Inside the dark hollow Raymond found his cloth bag lying where he'd left it. He felt for the cold metal of the door handle and opened the door.

In the moonlight he could see hundreds of Weeuns around the entrance to the underground passage. They stood bewildered, lost, so tiny that Raymond felt a twinge of sadness.

The underground passage here was filled with rocks and dirt, the same as at the other end. Dust still hung fine in the air. The Weeuns turned helplessly to each other, or stared at the collapsed underground passage. A few moved in aimless circles, their bodies bent forward, rushing nowhere.

Raymond looked down to see Miffit, the red-haired Weeun, standing at the bottom of the Gartergates. He stood sadly, dejected, filled with great pain.

"You have done a hard thing," Raymond said.

"It had to be," Miffit said, his voice barely reaching Raymond.

Raymond held out the cloth bag he'd left in the hollow. It was filled with seeds of the good edible plants that

191

grew in Waterpushin but not in the land of the Weeuns, of plans for bringing water up into the gardens and better ways to grow things.

He was about to drop it down, but then pulled it back inside the hollow. He took the silver Tiny of the Garter-gates from his pocket. For one last time, he felt the rough words, FOR TRUE, on the back of the Tiny, then he placed it on top of the neatly marked packets of seeds in the cloth bag and pulled the drawstrings securely shut. He dropped the bag down to the Weeun.

Miffit picked the bag up from the ground and held it in his arms. It was nearly as big as he was.

"What will happen now?" Raymond asked.

Miffit patted the bag. "With these we can grow the food we need to live." He waved a hand toward the silent group of Weeuns. "It will be hard. There is no leader now."

"There will be," Raymond said, picturing the red-haired Weeun giving the Weeuns a newer, better way of life.

"We will close off this door," Raymond told the Weeun. "It will never be opened again. It will be as if it never was."

"And the underground passage will never be re-opened," Miffit said.

"All that has happened will only be stories. There will be no way for anyone to prove it was for true."

"There can be no other way," Miffit said. "It is sad."

"Sad," Raymond repeated.

Miffit turned and walked toward the group of Weeuns, the bag clutched tightly to him.

"Good Gloom," Raymond called softly. But if Miffit heard, he gave no sign.

Raymond closed the door securely behind him.

EPILOGUE: The Celebration

*T*HE CELEBRATION lasted all night, a more joyful celebration than any Gloom Day. The square and cobbies echoed with laughter and singing and Bulkings congratulating one another.

Musicians were playing in the square, rollicking, happy music. Around them, some holding hands in long lines, some in circles, some by themselves, the Bulkings danced. Once, the musicians played the Fish Barrelers' song and everyone joined in, ending the song with a loud cheer for the Fish Barrelers.

Wicker Bugle's hand was taken freely. Her gray dress whirled through the crowds as she was swung and led through the dancers.

Even the Majester danced and laughed. No speeches this night.

Raymond and Bort sat on the cobbles by the Majester's old house. The images of the dancers swirled and blended under the lamps that surrounded the square. Raymond blinked his eyes and brought them back into focus: the tired, happy faces; the smudged and torn holiday clothes; Constable Dragit dancing past with Wicker Bugle.

Merrily came out of the Majester's old house and sat beside Raymond. There were babies and small Bulkings asleep on cloaks and blankets in the Majester's old house, and every little bit someone would go inside to check on them.

"Trillia just told me that they're moving back into the Majester's old house," Merrily said.

"What about the house on Majester's Hill?"

"That's the best part. It's going to be a new school and a museum, a place to keep the old and precious things of Waterpushin. And there will be a path cut from Majester's Hill to the Gartergates."

" 'And now remember the Gartergates . . .' " Bort recited.

"They won't be forgotten this time," Raymond said.

"Don't be forgetting Wicker Bugle's new book," Merrily reminded him. "She'll make sure no Bulking forgets."

"Do you think," Bort asked, frowning, "that if Wicker Bugle hadn't learned the secret language of Royal Bugle's last book we Bulkings would have battled the Weeuns?"

"Waterpushin was in danger . . ." Raymond began, but Merrily jumped up and took each of their hands.

"It doesn't matter now," she said. "It's over. Look, it's almost sunrise. Let's dance before we go home to sleep."

She pulled on their hands until they stood.

Raymond had never danced before. He felt foolish as Merrily and Bort began to turn and twist, taking him reluctantly along with them, into the dancing Bulkings. His legs were stiff and awkward.

Rain into rivers, Gos had said once about the past. It was over and couldn't be changed, but it must never be forgotten.

Raymond's legs loosened as he felt the music flowing through him. He glanced back to where he and Bort and Merrily had been sitting and saw his great-great's hat and Glom Gloom's crooky-staff.

The museum. He would put them in the new museum.

Raymond stumbled, and Bort and Merrily held him from falling. They laughed loudly, and Merrily said, "Raymond, you're dancing!"

Raymond laughed and spun the three of them faster.